THE ETHIOPIAN EXHIBITION

THE ETHIOPIAN EXHIBITION

D.N. STUEFLOTEN

BLACK ICE
BOOKS

BOULDER • NORMAL

Published by Fiction Collective Two with support given by the English Department Publications Unit of Illinois State University, the English Department Publications Center of the University of Colorado at Boulder, and the Illinois Arts Council

Address all inquiries to: Fiction Collective Two, c/o English Department, Publications Center, University of Colorado at Boulder, Boulder, CO 80309-0494

The Ethiopian Exhibition
D.N. Stuefloten

ISBN: Paper, 0-932511-85-6

Produced and printed in the United States of America
Distributed by The Talman Company

PART I
THE EXHIBITION

1
THE IRIDESCENT
<u>BIRDS OF ETHIOPIA</u>

On the Ethiopian plains, night falls at six o'clock. It is impossible to say with certainty why this is so. Later we shall discuss this more completely. Examples shall be given. In each case the horizon reddens. Stars appear. The last baboon climbs into his cave. The first hyena emerges from his lair. The diurnal birds—all of them are gray—fall silent. The nocturnal birds begin to sing. These nocturnal birds are brilliantly plumaged, even ornate. Their voices differ from those of the daytime birds. The daytime songs are as harsh as the countryside. They can be heard everywhere, even in the cities. The nighttime songs are seldom heard near human habitation. They are oddly melodious. Such songs can rouse unease. There are stories about some of these songs, and their effects on humans, that may be called incredible. Some of these stories will be discussed. This book may be seen as a discussion of these stories. No one alive today, however, can vouch for them. Perhaps no one alive today has seen a nocturnal bird. They are known, nevertheless, to have iridescent feathers. These feathers, however it is known, are said to be several feet in length. The eyes of these birds are said to be black and expressionless. These birds are capable of gliding soundlessly for miles. These birds are predators. They are most iridescent when hungry. There are tales of glowing birds carrying off children. We believe these stories are true. Infants vanish during the night. In daylight there is wailing. People gnash their teeth.

The bifurcation of Ethiopia between day and night is virtually absolute. In truth Ethiopia is two countries. It is rare for anyone—any man, any beast—to know them both.

2
THE FOUR
CYLINDER INDIAN

A plume of dust rises from the wheels of a motorcycle. The rider of the motorcycle is John Twelve. He is a ferengie—a foreigner. Carried on his motorcycle are specimen jars, notebooks, cameras, a small typewriter, and items of personal wear. On his head he wears a leather helmet and goggles. Already he is covered in dust. The motorcycle is a four cylinder in-line Indian. It is quite ancient. Its motor can be heard for some distance: thump-thump-thump-thump, thump-thump-thump-thump. He purchased it on the docks. Does it run? he asked the owner, a plump man wearing a fez. The plump man puffed and blew as though insulted. Yet he started the machine only with difficulty. There was no paint left on the machine. It was eaten with rust. No tread was on the tires. Spare parts would probably never be available, not even in Ethiopia. Yet the ferengie paid money for this machine, plus the leather helmet, the goggles, and some cracked saddlebags. It is into these saddlebags that he stuffs his equipment. More items are strapped across the gas tank.

All this occurs in daylight. As he rides across the Ethiopian plains, a plume of dust rises from his wheels. This plume of dust is visible in the distant villages.

Nearby a black Abyssinian on a white pony watches. He wears a shamma, a loosely draped garment. He looks towards the horizon. The sun is already low. The pony wheels. His hooves are delicate. Even at a trot they raise scarcely any dust and create scarcely any noise.

3
<u>DESPAIR</u>

He is overwhelmed suddenly by despair. There is no ready explanation for such a thing. It happens during the brief moment of twilight. He pulls off the road and puts his face in his hands.

At such moments it is his nature to question everything. He is a man alone. He has no family. Although he has his studies, it seems that everything else has deserted him. There is no purpose to anything, least of all his life. Bitterness sucks away his vital spirit. He feels emptied. Later we will spend more time examining his despair. We shall try to make his despair palpable. Perhaps if his despair is given dimension, and texture, and color—perhaps if we can discover the sound of his despair—perhaps then we may understand it. Or perhaps we will discover it is a canker that will never be understood, not in Ethiopia, not elsewhere; and never be healed, not by day, not by night.

4
THE RAGING
TRUCKS OF ETHIOPIA

It is dark. He lies in his sleeping bag. A tarp is spread from the branches of a thorn tree over him and his motorcycle.

When the trucks begin to pass it is not clear if John Twelve is asleep or awake. His face grimaces, but his eyes remain closed. The trucks whine and snarl and snap up the hills and around the curves. Few have mufflers. The noise is intense. The trucks seem endless. They start shortly after dark, and stop shortly before morning. In Ethiopia trucks travel only at night. Their headlights throw shadows which veer across the landscape. They are festooned with other lights—red and green lights, blue and gold ones. The trucks themselves are painted bright colors, sometimes many colors. During the day they are hidden. Only their wreckage can be found in daylight hours. Trucks go off the road and plow through trees and into cliffs, and sometimes villages. On some dangerous stretches of road there are wrecked trucks stacked one next to another. Families live in some of these wrecks: in the huge trailers, twisted or not, and in the cabs, still reeking of oil.

Lines of wash are strung from truck to trailer and trailer to thorn tree. Children play in the shadows. Children are born in the huge aluminum caverns.

But at night the trucks race through the countryside. The roads, deserted all day, fill with diesel rigs and gasoline rigs, with semi-trailers and doubles, loaded and overloaded with goods that we can only imagine. They roar and they howl. There is silence only briefly, after a crash. Broken glass falls onto sheet metal hoods. Air hisses one last time from the giant brakes. Perhaps blood drips. Then the howling of the engines begins again. The trucks rage all night, all night, until the Ethiopian dawn.

5
THE SHAPE OF DESPAIR

Despair follows him like a plume of dust.

This plume of dust rises from the wheels of his motorcycle and hangs in the air for miles behind him. The plume of dust is visible from villages some distance away. The Ethiopians who live in these villages stop their tasks to watch. They squat in the shadows of their mud huts. They see how the eddies of wind in the air above John's motorcycle give the plume of dust a shape.

John, on his motorcycle, is unaware of this. He is deafened by the thumping of his four cylinder, in-line engine. He is aware of the constant vibration which batters his body. He is aware of the struggle to keep his machine upright and in a straight line. He is aware of the dryness of the air on the Ethiopian plain, and the heat of the sun, and the buffeting of the wind. He is aware of his despair, but he does not realize it is taking a shape in the plume of dust which follows him. He does not realize his despair is taking the shape of a giant locust. The natives in the villages see the locust. They watch the mandibles take form, and the powerful legs, and the primitive wings. They are aware of the locust in their own lives. The locust has swarmed across their land stripping it of their crops. They know how difficult it is to kill a single locust, with its armored body. They understand the devouring hunger of the locust. The natives in the villages watch the locust take shape. They watch the yellow sunlight, as it mingles with the dust, turn the locust green.

John, on his motorcycle, is unaware of the locust following him in the plume of dust. He cannot see it poised above him. We see it. We cannot alter this. We can only watch, like the villagers, as despair takes the form of a giant insect in the plume of dust which follows John across the Ethiopian plain.

6

THE PHOSPHORESCENT ANALS OF ETHIOPIA

It is dark. Like an animal he burrows into the bushes. He pulls his sleeping bag over his face. The motorcycle next to him pings and hisses as it cools.

The other daytime animals have gone to their burrows also. They are replaced by nighttime animals. These animals have black, glittering eyes. They are feral creatures. They stalk each other beneath the wild fig trees, the tall acacias, olive trees with gnarled and bent limbs, bottle trees with their pulpy bark, and flowering magnolias. From above—from the vantage of a soaring Ethiopian bird—the earth seems covered with unceasing movement. This is especially true during the mating season. The females become phosphorescent. Their sexual organs glow. They circle through the bushes, followed by the males. The female rodents, ferrets, wild cats, including the spotted leopard, even the female hyenas glow. Their organs of sexuality glow. They produce a kind of incense, particular to each breed. The male creatures follow the females, sniffing at the glowing vulvas. Coupling occurs

18

after midnight. The phosphorescence increases. There is a rhythmic pulsing to this glow. The odors become as strong as crushed flowers. The male animals snarl and snap at each other. The females, odoriferous and phosphorescent, growl also. Their movements become jerky—short steps to the right, quick turns to the left. Sometimes they leave trails of phosphorescence, along which bound the males of their breed. When coupling occurs, the odors become even stronger. Trees blossom at this time. If there is a rain, the rain smells like perfume. Above all of this glide the iridescent birds.

John sleeps. Perhaps his sleep is uneasy. Images flash, with a phosphorescence of their own, in his brain. When the Ethiopian dawn arrives, with a cracking sound, like thunder, he sits up, gasping.

7
AN ETHIOPIAN STREET

John descends from the Ethiopian plateau and enters a town along the coast. It has a harbor. There are green trees in the central square. He takes a room in a hotel which overlooks this square.

The streets of this Ethiopian town are filled with children of both sexes, priests wearing white turbans signifying their high office, chiefs and grandees and other important officials wearing peaked caps and carrying scimitars on their hips, slaves, generally black and nearly nude, gun bearers and retainers and zebanias, who are private soldiers, and merchants in long djellabas. The only females, aside from the few children, are old. They are mostly beggars, and sit in doorways, counting beads. All of these people, except the slaves and the old women, are constantly moving to and fro and making noises. The old women, as we have said, sit in doorways. The slaves stand silently, often stork-like, on one leg.

John walks down the crowded street. He hears Arabic, Spanish, French and occasionally English words, all spoken loudly and rapidly. Bitches with rows of swinging teats, puppies with stiff hind legs, and mastiffs drooling down their jaws pass underfoot. The air is hot and dusty. Because there is only a narrow strip of flat land between the ocean and the hills, soon the street ends. It becomes a stairway. The stairway rises steeply and crookedly up the hill. Houses are stacked here, one on top of another. No engineer, no architect had a hand in them. The houses are made of mud bricks, concrete, wood, and stone, and no corner is square. Clothes are hung on lines from house to house. Doorways are low; windows have shutters across them. The stairs turn right, then left, and become narrower as John climbs upward. For a long time only children watch him. The children have bare bellies. They stand with fingers in mouths. They stand in every doorway and at every turning of the stairs.

8
THE BLAZING SUN
OF ETHIOPIA

The stairs turn left. John turns left, still ascending. Above, turning to her left, a woman descends.

It is late afternoon. The sun blazes. The whitewashed buildings shine in this blazing sunlight. It is not clear why this woman is descending an Ethiopian stairway during daylight. She is swathed head to toe. She is mostly swathed in white. Her veil is black. The tip of one shoe, as it descends to the next step, is black. It is pointed, like the triangular head of a viper. Perhaps the shoe is patent leather. We can see it descend, like the pointed head of a snake, to the step below. Everything except this pointed shoe, the veil, and her eyes is white. Her eyes, veil, and shoe are black. The eyes are iridescent. This iridescence is similar to the iridescence flies have when they cluster on a piece of raw meat. As the black patent shoe descends, it emerges more fully from the hem of the robe. The ankle is sheathed in black nylon, perhaps black silk. Like the eyes, like the shoe, like the veil, there is an iridescence to the ankle. Perhaps this iridescence is a trick of

22

the blazing sunlight.

The sun blazes down. The man and the woman stand at the turning of the stairs. They stand like this for some time. No one can say why she has appeared like this. Her iridescent eyes are visible. Except for these eyes, the black veil, the black shoe, and the black-sheathed ankle, she is obscured entirely by her white garments. Then she is gone. The sun continues to blaze. Perhaps she has turned and mounted the steps. Perhaps she slipped away, elsewhere. John stands in the blazing sun, above his own shadow. Then he moves, too. He leaps up the stairs. He finds only low doorways, a slinking dog, and two children, naked and dirty, sucking at their fingers.

9
THE ETHIOPIAN WIND

A breeze rises from the sea. It moves inland. It tugs at John's clothes.

He looks down at the harbor and the tin roofs of the town. He can see camels moving in the streets, and mules, horses, a few ancient motorcars. Three ships are tied at the dock. Train tracks run from the docks alongside a lagoon and then westward, into the hinterland. The train itself arrives weekly, bearing grain, scrap metal, sugar cane, and slaves. All are sent overseas, the grain being traded for bread, the scrap metal to return as rifles and cheap watches, the sugar cane processed into Coca Cola. Only the slaves, we understand, remain overseas, in the kitchens of restaurants in Paris, Brussels, and New York.

John climbs higher. His shirt is dark with sweat and clings to his skin. The breeze is moist and hot. It causes the wooden shutters on the windows of the small, crooked houses to clatter. Doors creak back and forth in their doorways. The sheets of tin which form roofs clang as the wind from the sea lifts them and drops them. These are the only noises except for John's breath. John's breath is like the wind, moist and hot. For a moment, while John climbs, the wind and his breath are the same. This can happen in Ethiopia. The Ethiopian wind rises from the sea, just as humans rose from the sea. No man can remember the primitive sea, but his cells remember. His bones remember. When this wind joins with a man's breath there is a moment when these cells, these bones, rejoice. The man feels this as a moment of joy. The moment passes quickly. When the elation is gone, a sadness remains. This sadness is just as deep as the joy. It penetrates into the bones. The body aches in memory of the primitive sea. This is why a man forever yearns to penetrate into the womb of a woman. A woman's womb is saline, like the sea. The male organism, when it penetrates into the womb, recognizes this. Elation and sadness inevitably follow this recognition. These secrets are known in Ethiopia. They have been known ever since the wind first rose from the sea and blew across an Ethiopian town.

10
IN ETHIOPIA A WOMAN'S MOUTH IS A SEXUAL ORGAN

There is a face at a window. It looks down over the bay. It looks down over the steps that John is climbing.

In Ethiopia a woman's mouth is considered a sexual organ. Only young girls are allowed to be seen unveiled, in the same way young girls and boys are allowed to be seen nude playing in the streets. At a certain moment a girl's erotic nature becomes apparent. This event is obvious to anyone within view. Men dream of witnessing this event. If a man witnesses this event, he has a right to carry the girl off. The event may occur at any time, day or night. Forever after this moment, she must wear clothes and a veil and cover her hair, which is erotic also. Except for rare circumstance she will not be seen again in daylight, even thus garbed, until she is very old and her sexual power has waned. This is because the erotic power of the Ethiopian woman is so great. Her presence in the streets would prevent the Ethiopian male from performing his proper duties, which are thieving, lying, cheating, and murder.

The woman in the window watches as John mounts the steps. When he looks up, he sees her. He sees her just as the Ethiopian wind, warm and moist from the sea, lifts the corner of her veil. Her lips are dark red and fully engorged with blood. The lips draw back as the mouth opens. The teeth are exposed. The fleshy tongue lies across the lower row of these teeth. Deeper within the mouth is the phosphorescent glow of this sexual organ. This glow expands outward with the woman's breath. As this happens, her hand reaches for the wooden shutter of the window. The tips of her fingers are sheathed in long nails. Two of these nails are carved from bamboo; one is silver; the other brass, and encrusted with jewels. They taper to sharp points. The hand, thus sheathed, grasps the edge of the wooden shutter. All this takes place in seconds. Her lips draw back, engorged and heavy with blood. The mouth becomes fully extended. Deep in the throat emanates the phosphorescent glow. This glow begins to pulse. The sheathed fingers grasp the edge of the wooden shutter and draw it closed.

Immediately the wind from the sea dies.

11
THE WEIGHT OF DESPAIR

In Ethiopia the air has a weight. Normally no one is aware of this. When the air is very still, however, this weight may be tangible. It may be felt as the weight of despair.

This weight is composed of the dying exhalations of men, women, and children. Whenever a man is murdered, his last breath adds to the weight of the air. Whenever a child dies at birth, the passing of his soul adds weight to the air. The pain of his mother, although it may not be visible in the air, adds weight. During times of war, when villages are destroyed, and whole cities, and sometimes whole races, the increase in the weight of the air can cause a man to stagger. Not all men are aware of this. Cruel men are not aware of the weight they are adding to the air by each cruel gesture. In many countries this weight is taken for granted, and the people think nothing of mass bombings, or mass exploitations, or mass cruelties. Often if such people come to Ethiopia they feel, if not the weight of the air, a vague oppression. The weight of the air, which they have helped increase, gives them unease. They ascribe this unease to the sight of begging children or the dirt on the streets or the careless way food is prepared for them. But in truth it is the weight of the air, which they do not wish to feel.

When John reaches the top of the stairs, he is bent nearly double by the weight of the air. He staggers to the wall of a ruined building. He sinks weakly into its shade. The weight of human suffering is so great in the Ethiopian air that he is scarcely able to breathe it.

12
THE PARIAH DOGS
OF ETHIOPIA

In Ethiopia a man in a weakened state will be attacked by creatures eager to respond to that condition. In Ethiopia this is a natural law. The creatures that now come forward to attack John in his weakened state are pariah dogs.

Pariah dogs live on the fringes of all Ethiopian towns. They live in ruined buildings, in groves of trees that have fallen into disuse, and in the refuse pits that encircle even the smallest village. These pariah dogs, in response to John's weakness, come forward in a half circle around him. Their heads are low to the ground. Their ears lie flat. Lips are drawn back to reveal canine fangs. More emerge from doorways, from holes in the crumbling walls, and leap down from windows. If we watch the scene from above, we may admire its classic simplicity. The setting is perfect. The sea at this hour is jewel-like. It is clear and pure as an amethyst. The ruins where John and the pariah dogs enact their drama are on a promontory overlooking this sea.

In Ethiopia the pariah dogs, although not liked, are

expected to perform their role with honor. The tragedy they sometimes bring is the price one pays for being a member of the larger drama of all living things. The frenzy of the pariah dogs, when they rip into their victim, tearing off arms, chunks of flesh, scrambling amongst themselves for choice bits of entrails, liver, or spleen, is not seen as an aberration but as an example of the ferocity which exists in nature, and which thus needs expression. It can no more be avoided than the Ethiopian air, or the fall of night, or the lonely cries of a grieving widow. John, a ferengie, is unaware of the larger nature, or even the classic lines, of his role. He does not understand what every Ethiopian knows, that when confronted by pariah dogs one must exhibit either resignation or dominance. The signs of resignation would signal the pariah dogs to attack. The signs of dominance would signal them to flee. John's posture is that of a frightened man, which provokes the pariah dogs to attack, and yet he fights, swinging his arms, kicking out, which frustrates their attack. Because of this confusion, the pariah dogs mill about. They snap and snarl, dart in, then retreat. John, backed against the mud brick wall, lashes out. The confrontation cannot come to a satisfactory conclusion. The pariah dogs howl and cry in frustration and anger. In the town below, people hear these cries, and pause.

Night falls. The pariah dogs, creatures of the day, slink off into their burrows, their nature wounded. John, a ferengie, a misfit in the Ethiopian landscape, is abandoned to the Ethiopian night.

13
THE SONGS OF
THE ETHIOPIAN NIGHT

It is dark. John Twelve stands alone in the darkness.

He walks through the darkness to the edge of the cliff. He finds his way slowly. He stops when he feels the earth crumbling at his feet. Below him is the town. In the center of the town is the square. The square is full of trees. The trees, in the darkness, are beginning to flower. In Ethiopia the trees flower only at night. As the flowers emerge they begin to glow. Below these flowering trees small animals scurry. The vulvas of the females of these animals glow. All have iridescent eyes. Soon this glow, the glow of the female vulvas and the flowers opening on the trees, is visible from the top of the promontory where John stands. It is at this moment that the nocturnal birds of Ethiopia begin to sing.

They sing as they pass over John's head. They descend from high in the night sky. Their glowing wings are outstretched. Their tips especially glow. Some of these wings are enormous. As these Ethiopian birds glide past John's head, he can hear the wind rushing through the glowing feathers.

He can feel the wind they create as they pass over his head. The music of these birds is so soft it seems palpable. One could sink one's hands into these songs. One could rest one's head on these songs, just as one could rest one's head on the soft breast of the bird itself. As each bird, descending from high in the night sky, glides over the head of John, its soft song glides over him also. It becomes louder, though no less soft, as the bird approaches. It becomes more distant, though no less beautiful, as the bird glides to the square below. The beauty of each of these songs passing over John's head is unbearable. That is, these songs cannot be borne in the way normal songs are borne. That is the great danger of these songs. They enter into a man's blood. They invade his bones. They will forever ache behind his eyes, at the hinge of his jaw, at the base of his spine. It is a kind of pain. There is no relief from it. As the birds glide over John's head, singing, singing, to the square below, he can feel the softness of each song as clearly as he feels the soft wind of their passing.

14
THE WOMEN OF
THE ETHIOPIAN NIGHT

It is dark, perhaps very dark. From all sides women emerge from this darkness. They are visible in the glow which they themselves cast. Their eyes are iridescent. Each mouth pulses with its glow. A glow emerges from the center of each body. The women come out of the darkness and walk towards John at the edge of the cliff. They do not look at him. They walk towards him and towards the edge of the cliff.

The women are no longer swathed head to toe. They wear fine silks. They wear thin veils and tight dresses. They are garbed in finery from all over the world. Much of their bodies is revealed. Some are almost nude. They step forward in translucent garments. They step forward in high heeled shoes that are iridescent in the darkness. They step forward on legs that shine, sheathed in silk. As these women step towards John, towards the cliff, they make a murmuring noise. It is not clear if this murmuring noise emerges from between the lips on their faces or from the lips, visible or not, that glow between their legs. The murmur is as soft as the songs of the Ethiopian birds. The sound envelops John. The women, murmuring and glowing, walk towards John, walk past him, to the edge of the cliff. They do not pause. They spread their arms and leap into the darkness.

15
THE EDGE OF THE CLIFF

It is dark. John watches the women emerge from the darkness. At the edge of the cliff they spread their arms. John watches their glowing forms descend to the square far below. They join the glowing flowers and the glowing animals and the glowing birds which have come to roost there. They circle, some to the left, some to the right. They go round and round. John watches.

The last woman emerges from the darkness. She pauses at the edge of the cliff. She is the only one to do this. Her iridescent eyes turn. They turn to look at John. Her lips, engorged with blood, draw back from her teeth. The mouth becomes fully extended. The glow that emerges from deep in her mouth begins to pulse. She says nothing, but there is about her a murmuring sound. It is not certain what this sound means, or if it means anything. The iridescent eyes themselves contain no expression. They stare at John. She wears black shoes with high heels. Her legs are sheathed. She pauses at the edge of the cliff—she is the only woman to do so—and stares with her iridescent eyes at John. She stares at him while her mouth is fully extended. Then she spreads her arms. She leans forward into the darkness. She glides to the square far below.

16
INTO THE DARKNESS

It is dark. The glowing Ethiopian woman spreads her arms. John watches her descend. Soon her glow is indistinguishable from the others circling right and left in the square. He watches from the edge of the cliff. There is nothing luminescent about him. We can see no glow coming from his mouth or his body. He stands in darkness. The luminescence is far below. He watches it. Then he steps to the edge of the cliff. The earth crumbles at his feet. He spreads his arms. This can only happen once. He stands in darkness far above the luminescence. There is nothing luminescent about him. He spreads his arms and takes a step forward. The earth beneath him crumbles. The earth beneath him gives way as he leans forward into the darkness.

17
FAITH

It is dark, perhaps very dark. A flower from a tree hangs in the damp air. The flower glows. Luminescence fills the Ethiopian night.

Daylight arrives. The square is empty. Then it fills with murderers and thieves, with petty cheats and foolish liars. They mill about. The sun blazes. It is a daytime world in which everything is visible. There are no secrets. There are no mysteries. We pass down streets made filthy with garbage. Men drop their feces in alleys. Dogs slink from shadow to shadow. The sun blazes on all of them. Cracks spread through concrete walls. Rust eats at the tin roofs of the houses. In the blazing sun even the shadows are harsh. This harshness cannot be avoided. We pass through it. The sun dips towards the horizon. It blazes onto the ocean. We watch the shadows lengthen. Perhaps we can hear a distant murmur. As the sun falls, there is a suggestion of luminescence in the air. It cannot quite be seen, but we have faith it is there. Night will come. In Ethiopia, night will always come. We must believe that. Night will come. We will await it.

PART II
<u>THE COMMENTARY</u>

1. *On the Ethiopian plains, night falls at six o'clock*. And ends at six in the morning. The few minutes of twilight are perfectly balanced. The *equivalence* between day and night is exact. We understand this is not true in other countries, and that the comparative relationship between day and night changes. Why this should be so is not clear. Alfonse de Llovia (*My Life and Observations*, 1653) suggested the lack of balance in other countries was inherent and endemic. That is, the lack of balance exhibited itself in all aspects of the lives of these people. Elehui Cardin claimed to have found seventeen "points of imbalance" in a single composition of music by Johann Bach ("The Etudes of Dissonance," *Proceedings of the Royal Society*, 1912), and we ourselves have argued ("A Theory of Imbalance," *Proceedings*, 1983) that a whole series of dissonances may be postulated from the single fact of this diurnal-nocturnal imbalance. That John Twelve himself had some inkling of this is apparent from the notes he left. He writes them in a rude cafe at the side of a dirt road. The cafe is run by an old woman. She tells him freely that she has had eighteen children, of whom nine died before they were five years old. She squats at his table. Outside the sun is very hot. Three Ethiopian men, already drunk, stand behind him. They watch him make his notes. His handwriting is crabbed, tiny. One of the drunks stabs at the paper with his finger.

"What you do?"

His words are so slurred John cannot understand him.

"What you do? *There!*"

"I am writing," John says with the impatience of one explaining the obvious.

"Why you do that?"

"Why?"

The question seems to annoy him. He bends over the paper and writes the word: WHY? Above this word, so large and dark, are the notes about dissonance. The words sprawl across the page, almost unreadable. We have deciphered them with difficulty. *I dreamed last night,* he had written, *I was walking with a group of women. They would not talk to me.* John Twelve, unlike most of his countrymen, was not unsophisticated about metaphor. The meaning of his statement, which the rest of the dream (taking up nearly a third of the page) merely explicates, is clear. The large WHY? below is almost an excessive ornament.

"You journalist?" the drunk demands of John ("Periodista arre?"). He is leaning now across John's right shoulder. His dark finger has left its imprint on the white paper.

"Journalist?" John replies with irritation. "No—scholar."

"Journalist!" says the drunk.

He picks up the paper. It collapses in his hand. The white edges of it stick out from his fist.

"Journalist!" he repeats. He spits onto the dirt floor. The ancient woman—the fat little gnome—giggles. The white paper flying through the air seems to amuse her. All of them laugh uproariously. John pays for his coffee and leaves.

2. *...the owner, a plump man wearing a fez.* The man in the fez, Dar bin Saleh, was actually a thief, and not the owner of the motorcycle. That was why he had difficulty starting the machine. The real owner—insofar as it had a real owner—was a dark, wiry Abyssinian, who watched the transaction from the shadows. His name was Ahmed. He was a murderer. It was his profession. He did not interfere with John's purchase. He watched the money change hands. He then followed Dar bin Saleh and garroted him in an alley behind the Hotel Savoy, taking the money, bin Saleh's wristwatch, and his fine leather belt. Afterwards he went to the police. He reported the motorcycle stolen and gave the sergeant five Maria Theresa dollars to purchase their action. In this manner he hoped to profit twice, in effect, from the occasion.

The day is hot and sultry. John Twelve parks the Indian motorcycle in front of the Hotel Savoy minutes after Dar bin Saleh, followed by Ahmed, passes it. A policeman strolls by later in the day, but he has not yet been advised of the theft: the five Maria Theresa dollars are not enough to make the sergeant act in haste. In Ethiopia police subsist on bribes, with the amount of the bribe determining the amount of action. They are paid no salary—a great savings to the municipal body—but are expected to earn their keep by the same system as all other Ethiopian males, that is, by lying, cheating, thieving, and murder. In Ethiopia the police mesh perfectly with their society. John Twelve, in his room, knew none of this. From his balcony he could look down at the huge motorcycle. He had expected to purchase a mule or other beast—perhaps a camel—for his journey across Ethiopia, and considers the motorcycle a stroke of luck. That evening he sits at his desk, in the yellow glow of a kerosene lamp, and fills the first page of his notebook with his careful, tiny words. We have read them. His innocence is startling. As F'centa said, in a different context, "Reality has evaded them; they have yet to imagine the horrible truth of their existence."

3. He is a man alone. So too was Ahmed. Murderers are by nature loners, but in Ahmed's case the aloneness was complete. His father, also a murderer, had been killed by his uncle, the great Afaq Torquemond. Of Ahmed's six brothers, three had died of natural causes—typhoid, malaria, and dysentery, respectively—and three had been murdered. Ahmed had murdered one himself, not long after killing his father's uncle. There is often this incestuous quality in families of murderers. Ahmed's three sisters all died young. One was run over at age four by a Mercedes Benz, which was considered something of a distinction. One died at fifteen, while producing Ahmed's stillborn child. The other was murdered by Torquemond, the same uncle who murdered their father. Afaq Torquemond was quite famous. He carried murder to an exemplary extreme. He is reputed to have killed nearly fifty people. This does not put him in the same league as political leaders, who sometimes kill, anonymously, using orders written on slips of paper, many millions of people, or company presidents whose factories produce the pollutants and weapons that maim and kill other millions. Nevertheless, in the sphere of which we speak, Ahmed's father's uncle was considered exemplary. It is difficult to murder many people when you must do it individually, face-to-face, as it were, using primitive implements such as knives, garrotes, bludgeons.

Ahmed was thus quite alone. He had coffee some mornings with friends—other murderers—but their relationship was always marked with wariness. Their common pursuit drew them together, but one does not, at risk of one's life, let down one's guard in their company. In any case, even among murderers, he was something of an outsider. He was a thoughtful man, and a literary one. This thoughtfulness is unusual among Ethiopian men in general, and particularly so among murderers. Murder is not an action that one can examine with equanimity. It was Ahmed's burden to be a murderer who reflected on his actions. This quirk in his character caused him considerable pain, but it was a pain he bore with dignity.

Early one morning Ahmed watches John mount his—Ahmed's—motorcycle. The engine thumps loudly. The cracked saddlebags bulge. Another bag is tied across the gas tank. John pulls the leather helmet over his head and buckles it in place. The goggles make his eyes huge. He glances over his shoulder—he does not notice Ahmed—and starts down the road. Ahmed, with the peculiar liquidity which marks his movements, strolls to the bus station.

4. He lies in his sleeping bag. A Camp 7 sleeping bag, rather soiled, purchased in Long Beach, California two years earlier. Ahmed, on the other hand, steps out of the Hotel Puerto Vallarta.

He has dressed for the occasion in a loose silk shirt and gray slacks. He wears gray leather shoes and no socks. He appears casually elegant. Because of this, he stands apart from the crowd of Americans and Canadians who fill the boulevard. The Americans, Canadians, and occasional Australians are dressed in resort wear. Resort wear consists mostly of flowered shirts in shades of purple, orange, and yellow, and short baggy pants. The faces, arms, and legs of these Americans and Canadians are bright red. Some have peeling skin. The fatter women have dimpled thighs. The thinner ones, because of the way resort clothing is cut, appear spindly. Ahmed passes through them like a sleek leopard among cows.

5. John...is unaware of this. A murderer, on the other hand, must be aware of a great many things, simultaneously. That murderers have heightened awareness has been suggested by Arbent Kan, Delorio Santez, and H.P. Hentessy. A successful murderer neither drinks alcohol nor smokes tobacco or opium. The alertness of murderers is legendary. Afaq Torquemond once saved the life of a minister of state when he detected, out of the corner of his eye, the moving shape of a rifle muzzle 300 meters away, deduced instantly who the intended victim must be, and with casual ease interjected a bystander into what he judged to be the line of fire. Torquemond, as every Ethiopian knows, then dispatched the minister himself—when a man is meant to die, he is meant to die—but did the job the way a murderer is supposed to do it: close at hand, in this case with an icepick thrust between the ribs and into the minister's heart. The gunman was set upon by a crowd and torn limb from limb. In Ethiopia, the proprieties are to be observed.

As Ahmed walks from the Hotel Puerto Vallarta and through the throngs of tourists, he observes them all. He notes marriages in disarray, affairs beginning and ending, teenagers glazed with drugs; he sees slack jaws and even slacker eyes; the marks left in the flesh by too many whiskeys, too many fatty foods, too many sweets, steroids, and sexual failures. Out of long habit he singles out the faces of victims and those about to become victims. He is not intending to murder anyone—he has killed recently, after all—but a murderer's skills are never quiet. He must use these skills constantly, not only to hone them, but to protect himself. A murderer is always fair prey to another murderer. Murderers, in fact, and victims, are separated by a fine line. Ahmed has pointed this out himself in his elegant monograph. *Your face is mine,* he wrote. *I see you as I see myself in a mirror. That is how I recognize you.* A murderer in Ethiopia, of course, cannot murder just anyone. He can only murder a victim. In this respect he is like the pariah dogs. He too is an outsider. He functions at the edge of society and does not belong to it. He is a predator, not a herd animal. His evolutionary job is to cull the herd and to assist those rare people wise enough to seek out their own death.

But if he is not searching for a victim to murder, he is nonetheless searching. Later we will explain why. Finally he slows his pace. He comes almost to a stop. He drifts across the street, slipping between the crowds of trucks and taxis and jeeps filled with over-fed, over-blond youths. He is stalking. When he stalks, he is virtually invisible. The red and white tourists do not notice him. He is a shadow flowing over the sidewalk. When he is satisfied, he slips behind his prey.

"Mademoiselle?"

He has touched her shoulder. She turns. Her eyelids lift, slightly.

"Yes?"

The single word dooms her.

6. It is dark. Night has fallen in "Puerto Vallarta" as well. This town, gathering American dollars from millions of tourists, is the principal source of hard currency for Ethiopia. The name of the town changes regularly, according to agreement with a certain Latin American country. Next week the town will become Cancun, and the week after that, Las Hadas. When night falls in this town, daytime activities do not entirely cease. There is not that precise division which bifurcates the rest of Ethiopia. Thus while John sleeps, surrounded by the glowing animals of the Ethiopian night, in Puerto Vallarta the streets are still filled with foreign tourists. Lights, not animals, glow in the hotels and restaurants and discos. Lamps hover over the street, attracting swarms of flying insects. However, the Ethiopian night does leak into the town. All the electrical power from the humming lines cannot entirely keep it out. This is apparent to even a casual observer. The town seems harsh and dry during daylight. When day is gone, the town acquires a kind of charm, perhaps even beauty. The tourists themselves, graceless as they are, notice this. They talk about the nights in Puerto Vallarta. Or Acapulco. Or Ixtapa. They are not aware that they are talking about the magic of the Ethiopian night.

Things that are inconceivable during daylight hours become possible at night. Only an Ethiopian like Ahmed is aware of this. He touches the shoulder of his prey.

"Mademoiselle?"

"Yes?"

Her eyelids lift slightly, then descend. But the rising and lowering of these eyelids has taken place at the exact moment when daylight becomes night. At that moment her soul is illuminated, and the vision thus created cannot be rescinded. Her single word, the single "Yes?" is spoken at the same moment and likewise cannot be rescinded. Nor can the actions which follow. Moments later she is in his room. Her pants are on the floor. She is bent forward, leaning over a chair. Ahmed spears her from behind. Although her vulva does not glow—she is not an Ethiopian woman—it possesses a satisfying warmth. She is very young, scarcely more than a child, and quite slim, but there is already that dimpling at her thighs that seems to plague American women. Her legs nonetheless are certainly beautiful, especially in the pale light from the window. Ahmed's room is high above Puerto Vallarta; from the window—she now leans against its sill, still bent over, still receiving Ahmed's sexual organ—she can see the long line of vehicles moving in the streets below and the disorganized throng of people moving on the sidewalks. All are illuminated by yellow light. The yellow light rises through the air and dimly illuminates the girl's young breasts. Her shirt, adorned with a pale purple flower, lies on the bed next to Ahmed's trousers. When she lies on the bed, next to this shirt and these trousers, her legs are over Ahmed's shoulders. He holds one of her ankles in his hand. His body is arched. As she looks up at him, her eyelids drop even lower. Her mouth, which is slackly open, bears faint traces of lipstick. The lips are bruised. They are thus engorged with blood. The lips of her vulva are likewise engorged with blood. Her liquids may be seen on Ahmed's mouth and, transferred from there, around her mouth as well. When her legs are lowered, her heels hook around his ankles. There is a symmetry to their positions. At that moment she takes a deep breath.

The moon has risen. Its yellow glow joins the yellow glow that spills onto the sidewalk from the windows of the shops and restaurants of Puerto Vallarta. Ahmed offers his arm. The girl takes it. She is wearing now a dress, although it is not clear where this dress came from. It is the exact color of twilight. The hour is late; it may be very late. Few people are about. Ahmed leads the girl into what appears to be a restaurant, or perhaps a nightclub. Three people await them at a table. They are Haile Selassie, Sheba Makeda, and Prester John. Of the three of them only Sheba, who has been dead more than 3,000 years, can speak. She looks like a bejeweled hyena.

The girl says her name is Sandi—with an "i."

"That is impossible, my dear," says Sheba. "I would like to be kind to you but a name like that is inconceivable. I wont have it on a marquee. I shall give you a name. Provisionally, of course. What do you think of 'Dominique?' "

The girl gives Ahmed a sidewise glance.

"Dominique?" she says.

"Provisionally, of course. What do you say, Ahmed? Is she a domina*tor*—or a domina*tee*?"

Her mouth nearly unhinges with a bray of laughter. Her teeth are yellow stubs. Haile Selassie, next to her, winces. The Queen of Sheba, dead 3,000 years, has terrible breath. Even Dominique, across the table, must draw back from it. She says nothing, however, about this coarse display. Her gaze lingers on Sheba's fingers, each adorned with a rare and precious stone. There is gold strung around her neck. Diamonds hang from each ear. The leopard skin coat, askew on one shoulder, has a broach on which Dominique counts fifteen emeralds, each larger than ten carats. Sheba's open-toed pumps are festooned with rubies. A yellowed toenail—it curves beyond the tip of the shoe—has a sapphire glued to it. Many of these jewels are coarsely faceted. They are uneven in shape. Nevertheless they glow even in this dim room. There is a nimbus of light around this creature. When she leans forward, her fat breasts, insecurely housed in her evening gown, flop onto the tabletop. There are rubies in the folds of her flesh. Dominique's eyes, always hooded, become even more secretive. She crosses one nylon-sheathed leg over the other.

"What's the movie about?" she asks.

Her voice is breathless.

❖

She stands on the stage. A single spotlight illuminates her. Perhaps they are in a nightclub after all. She turns slowly. Although there is no music—there is no sound in the room except the whir of Prester John's Panavision camera—perhaps she is imagining music.

"The film," Ahmed says at last—he is still at the table—"is about the delusionary nature of reality."

The girl turns, and turns.

"The delusionary nature of what we call reality. Or perhaps, my dear, the real nature of delusion."

Sheba barks.

"Do not listen to him, dear Dominique. I will tell you what the film is about. It is about a man who foolishly—or am I being redundant?—a man who foolishly crosses Ethiopia. On a motorcycle, during World War II. A journey that can

only be described, if we must describe it, as the triumph of
delusion over reality. What else is a summer in Ethiopia?
Nowhere else is there such heat. Nowhere else does the sun
blaze with such fierceness. While bombers explode over
Europe, while Nazis march from triumph to defeat, while
Jews cook in ovens and children burn in Dresden, while
whole cities are turned into rubble, men into cripples,
women into whores—this man, this fool, straddles a four-
cylinder motorcycle and crosses Ethiopia—searching for
truth, for beauty, for reality! Who could imagine such a
thing? Only Ahmed, the great *directeur*, the *haute autor* who
dazzles us with images conceived out of the filth of the world!
A man who crawls—yes, my dear—a man who crawls through
the gutters of our souls to erect monuments to the splendor
of imagination! He smells of cordite, Dominique, he stinks
of TNT and the hot oil from the engines of tanks, he reeks of
the decay of flesh, of burnt limbs, of blood turning black in
the sun! And he promises us—listen to me, dear Dominique!—he promises us beauty and the purity of his vision! A
madman!" The girl turns, and turns. Although the camera
continues to whir, Prester John is no longer visible. Haile
Selassie has become a density in the air. Sheba brays once
more, spraying the air with jewels of spit. Then she too is
gone. Only Ahmed remains.

❖

"He put his hand on my leg."
"Who?"
"That man—"
"Selassie?"
"Yes."

"Ah."

"What does he do? On the movie?"

"He is the producer."

"And you—"

"The director."

"That woman—"

"The Queen. You must have noticed her jewelry. She is fabulously wealthy. She is the principal backer of the film. So she has, of course, special prerogatives. But dont let her put her hand on your leg. And I will speak to Selassie, although it will do little good. I will tell him your legs are mine to fondle."

"Oh...Shall I keep on turning?"

"Slip the dress off your shoulder."

"Like this?"

"Now let it slide to your feet."

"..."

"Precisely. Precisely, dear Dominique."

7. John descends from the Ethiopian plateau and enters a town along the coast. This plateau is the dominating feature of Ethiopia. Most of Ethiopia rises over 8,000 feet above sea level. In its physical features, Ethiopia rather resembles a hat. It is nearly surrounded by a narrow brim of lowland desert. The Rift Valley, like a crease in the crown of this hat, falls off to the south. Some of the central plateau is comprised of level or rolling plains—the Gojjan, for instance, and the Shoa plains—but much of it is broken by great canyons. These canyons are the largest and the steepest on earth, as many writers have attested. The Simian Highlands in the north are so broken with fissures that only one animal, the Walia Ibex, the most nimble creature alive, can live there. Nothing else can negotiate the sheer cliffs. The Abbai River—or Blue Nile, as we understand Westerners call it—has a canyon six thousand feet deep that is quite impassible. Aside from the Abbai, there are rivers like the Wabbi Shebali, which rises near Lake Abaya, and the great Hawash, which vanishes into the sands of Dankaliland. These Dankalis are lowland savages who kill all who enter their territory. Elsewhere Ethiopia is populated by Gallas and Abyssinians and Nubians. Slaves, mostly Nubians, are taken from the west, near the Arrusi escarpment. In the north central area are Portuguese castles built in the 16th century by Dom Cristoforo da Gama when he came to the aid of the Christian King Lebna Dengal.

Known in Europe as Prester John, he was being hunted like an animal by the army of the Musselman Mohammad Gran. When John descends from the plateau he skirts Dankaliland and passes near the area where Prester John once hid. The port town he reaches is on the shore of the Red Sea. The name of the town in English means little apples, although no apples are grown there.

The town is built in front of, up the sides of, and between two hills. The town faces a bay which provides good anchorage. Behind the town is a lagoon which extends several miles to the south. Once canoes skimmed this lagoon. Fishermen cast nets at night. Poets came to gaze at this scene, which was famous throughout Ethiopia. *The nets are sea spray/Fish made from moonlight/Gnarled hands do their work.* (*Da magan sen maganan/ Dashen sakan dashoi/Korganlagan da mogan dakoi.*) When Puerto Vallarta was built it had to be supplied with electricity. A generating plant was constructed on the edge of the lagoon to create this electricity, which until then was unknown in Ethiopia. In a single year the town of "little apples" tripled in size. A sewer line was built to the sea to accommodate this increase. When it collapsed—the cement was adulterated—the sewage poured into the lagoon, along with the waste products from the generating plant. Soon the sand around the lagoon turned gray. The fish died, and then all the plants except the hardy mangrove. In the center of the lagoon, where the waste from the town met the waste from the plant, the water boiled. A haze of selenium, lead oxide, and mercury vapor filled the air. The prevailing wind blew this haze into the city. Soon children were born deformed. They had incomplete faces. Six fingers became as common as five. Parents would have ten, fifteen, sometimes twenty of these children. Not all would live. Those who did could be seen walking single file down the streets, the ones who had eyes leading the ones who did not. Their parents garbed them in black. On Sundays they limped, they crawled, they were led, they were carried to the church, where the priest thanked God for the town's high level of employment, the highest in Ethiopia.

It is into this town that John Twelve descends. He stops at the outskirts to purchase gasoline. Children rush out to surround him. They carry rags which they wipe over his fenders. Their quick little hands dart into his luggage, looking for loose objects. John tries to wave them away, at first politely, then with desperation. The children grin at him, flashing teeth that are white, brown, and black. All this is on film, captured by Prester John's giant Panavision camera. The children have a single cry:

"Money!"

"Money!"

"Money!"

Gasoline bubbles and spits into the tank. The attendant takes advantage of John's distraction to charge him double and short-change him as well. From his packs John loses one of his cameras, a pair of shoes, and two bars of soap. The 2 1/2 gallons of gasoline he acquires thus costs him more than $600. Later Ahmed shows the "rushes" of this scene to Dominique, Sheba, and Haile Selassie. Prester John comes back and forth from the lab where he develops the film. They are in the same nightclub, or perhaps restaurant, as before, although it is no longer clear that this nightclub or restaurant is in Puerto Vallarta or in the town John has just entered. Dominique wears her twilight dress. Her legs are sheathed in black nylon. Her feet are shod in black patent shoes with spiked heels. On one finger she wears a sapphire. When the lights are dimmed, Ahmed puts his hand on her leg. After a moment Haile Selassie does the same. Dominique's hooded eyes watch the screen.

"Who plays the man on the motorcycle?"
"Does he look familiar?"
"Vaguely."
"You would know him by his stage name. In America he is a rock star. He calls himself 'Fang.'"

Fang grins at the camera. He mugs. He pulls back his lips to reveal his incisors, the incisors from which he takes his name. He is famous for his onstage antics. During his concerts he bites off the heads of small animals—bats, rats, and small cats. He sprays the blood from these animals onto the front rows of his audience. When a young girl—most of his fans are young girls—is sprayed with blood, she will faint. Her body will jerk orgasmically. She will not wash for weeks, until the mark—the blood—left by Fang has at last worn away. This is a tradition—that is, this has been going on for about a year, which is as long as most traditions last in America. The ecstasy he rouses has little to do with his music, which is mostly repetitive chords, or his lyrics, which are mostly obscene and blasphemous phrases spoken backwards, or his talents as a performer, which are ordinary. Marat Secord, the great Ethiopian analyst of foreign cultures, would doubtless call him a "releaser," a word he coined for another American singer of little talent. (See "Rudy Vallee: A Conspiracy of Hysteria," Proceedings, 1939.) Such "releasers" become the focus of the repressed sexuality of American girls. They are chosen almost at whim and are discarded as haphazardly. Some of these performers, like Fang, come to believe they are actually talented and that their talent is the reason for their popularity. When their popularity vanishes—often overnight—they blame producers, the media, politicians, agents, organized religion and organized crime, and in one instance, the fluoride in the drinking water. In truth they are simply following the immutable trail described a half century ago by Marat Secord, who analyzed the repression and attendant promiscuity of American girls.

On the screen, Fang, in the character of John Twelve, roars away from the gas station leaving a trail of dust. In this trail of dust an Ethiopian boy examines the shoes he has stolen. There is a bubo on his neck the size of a toad. He turns towards the camera and smiles sweetly.

"Will I meet him?"
"Fang? You will play one scene with him."
"One?"
"Just one. But it is a crucial one. Now watch this."
Prester John has threaded new film into the projector. Dominique appears. She turns, and turns, illuminated by the spotlight.
"Beautiful," Ahmed says.
Dominique looks at him out of the corner of her eye.

8. ...a woman descends. It was not a woman but a *gajjin*, or transvestite, in this case a young man named Julio Abril. Julio, expecting a busy afternoon, was dressed in his latest finery: French stockings and garter belt, shoes by Charles Jourdan, and brassiere and panties by Christian Dior. Beneath his white djellaba he wore a slick mauve cocktail dress, in the current mode, made by his mother. His breasts had been pumped up and his figure feminized by injections of lamb placenta. He was one of the stars of Le Club Mediteranee, a private organization frequented by politicians and wealthier businessmen. These gajjin are a recognized class in Ethiopia. They are trained to treat men in the way men treat each other, with flattery, lies, and petty deceits. Gajjin are famous for their skills at fellatio. Julio has been heard to brag that he ate so much sperm that he no longer took food. We cannot be certain that this is true.

Women plied the trade of prostitution too, but they were fewer in number and more atavistic in appearance. When John Twelve—or Fang, playing John Twelve—rode past the electric generation plant and along the lagoon, he passed three of these women. Each had her own tree. Shift workers from the plant lined up at these trees. John saw the lines of men, but did not notice the woman at the head of each line. Prester John's camera noticed, however. After each customer finished, the women bathed quickly in the lagoon, thus absorbing through their orifices lead, zinc, mercury, fecal matter, and other pollutants. Each charged half a Maria Theresa dollar, or about 25 cents in U.S. currency. By the end of a shift, this amounted to a goodly sum by Ethiopian standards. The women, however, seldom lived more than a year or two, usually dying of some form of cancer induced by the mercury or lead or other carcinogen in the lagoon. Of the three women at work on the day John Twelve passed, one was already near death. A tumor pressed visibly at her abdomen. Another's body was criss-crossed by surgical scars— a hysterectomy, an appendectomy, a colostomy, plus an exploratory incision which had exposed benign tumors in her viscera. The third girl was only thirteen, recently sold into service just as her sisters before her: their father considered daughters a harvestable crop. Just before the camera approached, this girl was seen applying lipstick and patting at her hair. As a man grunted over her, she turned toward the camera and smiled. The camera lingered for a moment on the happy face. When the man ejaculated, she slapped him playfully on his rump. Rather coquettishly she stepped into the water, her back turned to us, hands covering her breasts. Then she squatted, rinsed, and returned to work. The camera moved on. John, meanwhile, in the blazing sun, stares at Julio Abril. Dominique, at the same moment, sits at her dressing table. The room is cool and dusky. A lace garter belt encircles her tiny waist. Ahmed watches as she leans into the mirror to attach diamond earrings. They hang from the lobes of her ears like miniature chandeliers. In the mirror she sees Ahmed approach. Not now, she murmurs as he bends over her. Yet even as these words leave her mouth, the figure in the mirror rises to meet Ahmed. Dominique's eyes widen, perhaps in momentary alarm, and then half close into their habitual expression. The mirror is like a movie screen: she sees black hands enclosing pale breasts. She watches as the woman in the mirror exposes her neck to the black man's mouth. There is a genuine grace to her movements, and to his. Perhaps the scene will be accompanied by music. Doubtless the music will be sinuous. As white legs encased in black rise into the air—the tips of the shoes are iridescent—Dominique sees hands, perhaps her own hands, a diamond on one finger and a sapphire on another, pull at the tops of the stockings. Each stocking, stretched tautly, shimmers. The creature in the mirror throws back her head. Dominique can hear—everyone in the room can surely hear—the air sucking into her mouth. Ahmed's weapon—he is a murderer, after all—has penetrated the woman's body. Orgasm and death, in the mirror, are simultaneous. Perhaps they are identical. The music continues as the scene fades out.

9. *Only the slaves...remain overseas....* Many commentators have mentioned hearing Amharic spoken in the kitchens of Europe's finest restaurants. It is apparently difficult for those restaurants to hire native people to work the scullery. Ethiopian slaves, who are used to long hours at no pay at all, doubtless find the work easy.

Slavery is a venerable institution in Ethiopia. Prester John, when he was Lebna Dengal, King of Ethiopia, owned more than 10,000 slaves. He also had 1,000 concubines and a hundred wives. He had a hawkish nose, a barrel chest, and a virile member. He sired so many sons and daughters that people often refer to Lebna Dengal as the true father of Ethiopia. Today even beggars in Ethiopia claim to be descended from this prolific man. When he was forty years of age, he was converted to Christianity by a Jesuit. This was not as difficult as one might think. Christianity has had a long history in Ethiopia, and Judaism even longer. Moreover Lebna Dengal suffered from one severe flaw: he was an honest man. This was a great liability in his dealings with his own people, and an even greater liability when he began to reflect, as people often do at age 40, on the meaning of his life. He was also a man of great directness. He had used this trait to power himself into the kingship, to hew and hack and slice his way through all opposition. When he became a Christian, he put himself into the hands of Jesus. He was too honest, and too direct, to do otherwise. He released his 10,000 slaves into a labor market that was always uncertain. Freedom holds little meaning to most people, and none to most slaves, who found themselves begging on the streets and turning to thievery to sustain themselves. When provinces rebelled, Lebna Dengal, who now called himself Prester John, crossed himself and said he had faith in Jesus; Jesus was testing him. Prester John smiled at his advisers and took to wearing simple white clothes. He went for walks, blessing his subjects. Jesus will look after us, he said. We must put our faith in Him. At this moment in history, Islam began one of its periodic expansions. A Musselman named Mohammed Gran led an army across the Red Sea. Prester John laughed at his advisors' fears.

"Jesus is more powerful than an army of Musselmen," he said.

Prester John waited for miracles. The Ethiopian armies, lacking leadership, splintered into ineffective groups. The Moslems slaughtered, raped, and burned their way towards the capital. "We must put our faith in Jesus," Prester John declared again and again. Jesus would not allow the one Christian nation in Africa to be destroyed. Prester John fasted and prayed. He drank only water for fifteen days. He smiled peacefully at all who approached him. "Jesus told me not to worry," he said. "Jesus spoke to me. I feel certain he has great plans for all of us." Such was the force of Prester John's personality that people often believed him. He was an island of peace in a city torn with fear. He walked the streets, beaming at the panic-stricken people, blessing babies, calming mothers. He was in the streets when the army of Mohammed Gran burst into the city. They raced right past him. None of the Musselmen imagined this simple figure, heavily bearded, grinning, might be the King of Ethiopia. As his palace burned, Prester John stumbled from the city. His beard now was singed. There was blood on his hands, up his arms, and over his white clothing, from his ministering to the dying. He slipped and fell into a ravine full of thorn bushes. His clothes, his face, his body were sliced by the sharp thorns. He huddled against the cold. He could see in the sky the ruddy glow of his burning capital. He prayed all night. In the morning ashes floated through the air, like snow. The only visions that filled his head were visions of burning buildings, screaming children, horses rearing in panic, and corpses, piles of corpses, all leaking blood which ran in torrents down his streets. Prester John staggered off into the wilds of his country. For five years Mohammed Gran pursued him. Villagers hid him. He slept in caves. He ate bark and leather from his own boots.

A Portuguese army led by Dom Cristoforo de Gama landed in Massowa and allied itself with various Abyssinian chiefs. Da Gama was soon killed, but the Abyssinians and Portuguese, united under the new King Galaoudeous, took revenge against Mohammed Gran and at last drove the Musselmen from Ethiopia. Prester John was forgotten. He crawled down the escarpment near Dankaliland, subsisting on wild berries and competing with jackals for the rank carcasses of dead animals. He bathed in the Red Sea. Looking out over that great body of water, he swore an oath. Since his words had brought such suffering to his people, he would never speak again. To this day, alive and dead, bearded, face burnt and creased by the sun, flesh going slack on his arms and legs, eyes bright with anger, he has been faithful to his oath.

10. There is a face at a window. Ahmed's face was often at a window too. As a murderer it was his nature to be an observer. There was a voyeuristic quality to his life. Because of this it was easy for him to become a film director.

The film, like this book, is called *The Ethiopian Exhibition*. It is a series of images. It is entirely appropriate that the cameraman, Prester John, does not speak. In the late twentieth century only images speak. Words are dead. "In the beginning," says the Gospel of John, "was the Word." In the beginning words had power. They were mysterious. No one understood how words came into being or how they worked their magic. When bards like the blind Homer—he could not see, but he could speak—used their words to relate tales of adventure and mystery, people listened enthralled. They understood such words came from the gods. They understood words were sacred. Only people were blessed with the ability to say and understand words. Words remained sacred even when they were written down. Few people could read or write these words. During the dark ages in Europe, we understand that only monks retained the ability to read and write. This was entirely appropriate. But in the twentieth century, in Europe and the Americas and even parts of Asia, vast numbers of people were trained in this skill. Mass communication became feasible. This did not happen in Ethiopia, of course, where the true nature of words was always recognized. But in the rest of the world, when the mass of people began to read and write, words were quickly destroyed. Political leaders soon recognized that if a lie was repeated often enough, adamantly enough, widely enough, and in sufficient forms—in newspapers, in magazines, over radios and later television—people would accept it even if they knew it was false. Within a few decades words were debased everywhere. War Ministries became Departments of Defense. Invasions became incursions. Weapons designed to maim and kill were called Peacemakers. War was described as an action to protect the rights of the people it killed. Programs of assassination in occupied countries were said to be attempts to reach the hearts and minds of the inhabitants. Words were so debased that they ceased to mean anything. They were used finally only to sell cars, televisions, detergents, political platforms, tax plans, and as justifications for massacres. They were used only to avoid truth.

John Twelve explained all this to Ahmed. Ahmed, as a voyeur, as a murderer, recognized the debasement of words entering his country along with Coca Cola, electricity, and foreign ideologies. *The Ethiopian Exhibition*, John Twelve explained, would have to be a series of images. The book itself would use words only to create images. It would be an attempt to purify language of all deception. The movie would be the book in its purest form. No words would be spoken. Even the cameraman must not speak. The purity had to be rigorous.

They sat in a cafe overlooking a broad avenue in Addis Ababa. Gum trees lined the street. A Cord Cabriolet purred past, followed by a huge Packard with a veiled face at a rear window.

"I myself," said John Twelve, "will play the part of Fang,

playing me. And to add verisimilitude, I have imported a four-cylinder Indian motorcycle. It is on the docks right now."

Ahmed nodded. He suggested Prester John as cameraman.

"Excellent," said John Twelve. "Are we agreed?"

"We are agreed."

They shook hands. They ordered another round of *café au lait* and looked contentedly over the avenue.

11. When the air is very still...this weight may be tangible.
Perhaps John Twelve, standing on the parapet of Haile
Selassie's summer palace, can feel this weight. If so he gives
no indication of it. Instead he gazes down over the Valley of
Shoa. The steep sides of this valley are so barren, so gaunt,
that they could themselves be the symbol of despair. Yet
John Twelve does not appear despairing. He appears satisfied, perhaps even smug. We ourselves acknowledge his
accomplishments. He has traveled many thousands of miles.
He has overcome great difficulties. Perhaps he has a right to
be smug. He stands on the parapet of Haile Selassie's summer
palace, dressed in a silk robe, a cup of coffee in his hand,
listening to the sounds of construction rising, along with the
morning mist, from the valley below.

The cries of the workmen are as harsh as the cries of
Ethiopian birds. For six weeks these men have been at work.
Night after night trucks howled and snarled up the moun-
tainous road to disgorge lumber, bricks, slabs of concrete,
fixtures, and corrugated tin for roofs. Cobbled streets were
laid out. Houses rose up the hill, built one on top of another.
Although it all looked helter-skelter, it was carefully planned.
Engineers stood about with large maps and tape measures.
Surveyors shouted instructions. Foremen grumbled. No angle
was square, no line vertical or horizontal. Everything was
askew, except for the rails on which the cameras would run.

These rails were laid with great care. To save construction costs, many of the buildings were no more than false fronts. They were incomplete shells. How complete a building was—whether or not it had a roof or a third or fourth wall—was determined by the angle at which the camera caught it. This was all plotted on graphs, which the engineers carried. Windows that faced the cameras had shutters attached. Curtains were hung, and lanterns placed on rude tables. The nighttime trucks also brought loads of shrubs, bushes, and trees, which were placed around these buildings. The plaza itself took seven mature banyan trees, thirteen acacias, and twenty-nine flowering magnolias, plus hundreds of smaller plants. As John Twelve stood on the parapet of Haile Selassie's summer palace, workmen were putting the finishing touches—the last nails, the last sod—into place in this Ethiopian village.

12. ...the refuse pits that encircle even the smallest village. By
two o'clock these refuse pits began appearing around the
village below Haile Selassie's summer palace. An hour later,
when the caravan of vehicles passes, children are already
picking through the refuse. Thin gray smoke rises into the
air. Pariah dogs loiter in the shadows surrounding the refuse
pits.

Zebanias carrying muskets trot in front of the cars.

"Zourban!" they shout. *"Zourban!"*

In the second car—a 1936 Hudson Terraplane—Dominique turns to Ahmed.

"What are they saying?"

"They are telling people to get out of the way."

She peers through the window. One of her fine hands
fingers the mink pelt draped over her shoulder. She sees
children lining the street. Their dark faces smile. They hold
little flags which they wave in the air. Behind them are
schoolteachers, parents, and the shopkeepers who have
come out to wave also. The plaza in the center of town is filled
with people standing under the fine old banyon and acacia
and magnolia trees. A brass band plays in the bandstand. A
tuba goes *oompah, oom-pah-pah*. Policemen in pale green
uniforms and polished boots march back and forth. Other
policemen, fat ones, squat on Harley-Davidson motorcycles.
They wear black leather jackets and sunglasses, and stare

stonily at the crowds. Everyone else smiles, except perhaps for a few beggar women, who sit in doorways counting their beads, and slaves, thin, dark men who stand rather like storks on one leg. In the car ahead of Dominique and Ahmed—it is a fine old Dusenberg—Haile Selassie himself touches a hand to his braided cap. Otherwise he does not acknowledge the presence of his subjects. Seated next to him is Sheba. She periodically reaches into her purse, extracts a handful of pearls, and throws them out the window. Children scramble for these pearls as they bounce over the cobblestones.

Dominique stares out the window. There is a secret smile hovering about her lips, which are turned away from Ahmed.

"It's like a parade," she says.

"Isnt it?"

"Have they all turned out to see us?"

"They have come to see the Emperor."

Dominique turns slightly. Ahmed, in the gloomy interior of the Hudson Terraplane, is leaning back into the cushions. Dominique's eyes look cautiously in his direction. The light through the window illuminates half of her face, but none of his.

"The Emperor?"

"Haile Selassie. He was once Emperor of Ethiopia."

After a moment she says:

"Haile Selassie?"

"Yes. In those days he was called the Conquering Lion of Judah. He was deposed—oh, many years ago—in a revolution. But the people have never forgotten him."

The Hudson Terraplane purrs over the cobblestones. Children continue to wave their little flags. Dominique's eyes slip back towards Ahmed.

"Mr. Selassie was an Emperor?"

"The man you see, of course, is actually George Smithers, an actor from Pasadena. But he looks precisely like Haile Selassie. I doubt their mothers could tell them apart. He has the same tiny hands—and even the same taste for young girls."

"He's an actor?"

"Exactly."

"I thought he was the producer."

"That is true also. It is a multiple role, shall we say?"

He leans forward and taps the chauffeur on the shoulder.

"Come," Ahmed says. "Let me show you our village."

❖

Everything has been laid out as planned. Ahmed inspects the rails, which are like the rails of a miniature railroad. The camera, he explains, will run in a special carriage along these rails. He shows Dominique a chalk mark on the rail.

"It is here," he says, "that the camera will begin to rise. It will swoop into the air like a bird. All done hydraulically, of course. John Twelve—or Fang—will be across the street, half in the shadow of that building. This scene must be done at five o'clock, when the sun is precisely in position. As the camera rises, the rooftops become visible. That is why the rooftops, over there, are finished. You will notice that these buildings, on this side, possess only eaves. They have no backs as well. They are what we call false fronts."

Dominique stands a few paces from him. Her shadow falls obliquely to the ground. Her eyes are mere slits.

"You built this village?"

"A month ago it did not exist."

"Who were all the people in the street?"

"Extras, hired for the film."

When she follows Ahmed she remains the same few paces behind him. He sticks his head through a doorway.

"Empty," he says. "No back. Only rudimentary walls. While over there"—he nods across the street—"over there are shelves filled with canned goods. A kerosene lamp that actually works hangs from the ceiling. An ancient cash register with brass keys will be on the counter. A man could open that store—tomorrow. Would you like to see?"

She shakes her head.

"Ah," says Ahmed. "And here is the Indian motorcycle."

It is in a dark shed-like building. A near-naked man squats at its side with a glowing torch in his hand.

"This is the machine," Ahmed says, "that Fang will ride as he portrays John Twelve. Unfortunately the pistons are rusted. The whole engine is quite frozen. The motorcycle, you understand, is rare, and it has not been possible to obtain parts for it. So this man is attaching another engine, a small gasoline engine, to the right side of the motorcycle. The camera will always be on the left, so this engine will not be visible. A simple solution, yes? Of course the machine will not be able to go very fast, but speed wont be necessary. And the sound of the engine—well, these modern engines make noises like yapping dogs. But it will be a simple matter, in the studio, to dub in the deeper pounding of the original, four-cylinder engine." Sparks fly as the torch burns into metal.

"Ah. And there you see another pair of rails. These will carry the camera into an alley behind the Hotel Savoy, where a murder will take place."

"A murder?" says Dominique behind him.

"One must have drama in a film, mustnt one?"

He turns to her and holds out his hand.

77

"Come. Let us take some coffee, eh?"

❖

The cafe has rude wooden tables and chairs. A gnomish woman, dressed in black, waddles up. Ahmed orders two coffees with milk. Deeper in the shadows three men—perhaps they are construction workers—stare at Dominique. Their faces have the slackness of habitual drinkers, although they do not seem yet to be drunk. They murmur to each other, but make no move to interfere with the scene that now unfolds.

Dominique sits upright in her chair, lips pursed together, toying with her chipped cup. A sensitive observer—Ahmed, for instance—would recognize in her expression anger, uncertainty, and a trace of fear. It may be—it is probable—that she feels she has been taken advantage of in some obscure way. It would seem she has not been told everything relevant about this film. She has been allowed to assume things that were not, in fact, the case. Whatever secret pleasure she felt earlier, driven like a movie star, or a lady of state, past crowds of cheering children, has vanished. Perhaps in the aftermath of this elation she feels foolish. She is far from home, far from her family. She has put her faith in a man she hardly knows. The sun, falling towards the horizon, illuminates this man's face. It may be a sly face. The age of this face is indeterminate. The eyes are dark and seem to reveal nothing. He talks smoothly, perhaps in several languages. Perhaps he lies smoothly in several languages. It is probable that a movie is being produced, or at least contemplated; that much can be deduced from all the preparations. But the movie may not be what she was led to expect. Nothing is clear. Dominique was raised in a culture in which uncertainty is unacceptable. Americans, in fact, will accept the most blatant fabrication as an alternative to uncertainty. The easiest fabrication, as American politicians know, is xenophobia. Since it is her nature to be secretive, especially when filled with mistrust, she will say nothing, ask nothing, to clarify her position. She will watch through her slitted eyelids while people try to take advantage of her.

Ahmed sips with apparent pleasure at his coffee.

"My dear Dominique," he says. He spreads his black fingers and stares at them. "It is a great pleasure to work with you on this film. You must understand that as an artist I worship beauty. Beauty is my sole source of pleasure. That is why I create films. I am allowed—even paid—to take disparate elements, to take confusion and incoherence, and bring them to the highest order possible, the order of beauty. But such order, such beauty, is like a pearl. It requires a grain of sand around which to coalesce. In my art I think of this grain of sand as the Central Metaphor. It is the metaphor around which everything else gathers. In this film, my dear, and perhaps in my life—if you will allow me a deeply personal observation—you, Dominique, are the Central Metaphor."

Outside, children climb on board a bus. Flags litter the roadside. Black smoke puffs from exhaust pipes.

Someone—perhaps Dominique—utters a word:

"What?"

"I understood that, of course, the moment I saw you. As an artist I am trained to recognize metaphor." He gestures, open-palmed. "The film was dying. We were assembling elements, but nothing would fit together. You must understand my despair. I knew I had something truly exceptional here. This film—the possibilities of this film—were enormous. Money was invested, people were gathering from all over the world, equipment ordered, all was coming together—except in my own mind, where it all fell apart. Nothing would hold. We were in Puerto Vallarta, having a story conference. Everyone looked to me to explain what we were doing. I was speechless. Halfway through the conference, I could stand it no longer. I rushed outside. It was almost dark. I stalked the streets of Puerto Vallarta in absolute confusion. No, Dominique, in terror. If I could not create, out of all the resources given to me, I was lost. I had fallen into perdition. And then, my dear, I saw you."

13. It is dark. Actually it is twilight in the cafe. Ahmed chooses this moment to lean forward. He puts his hand on Dominique's leg. It is a gesture which can be interpreted many ways. For a moment Dominique struggles with her interpretation. Then her legs part, slightly.

Outside the cafe the Hudson Terraplane awaits them. The last bus has long vanished down the road, carrying the last child to the barracks—four barracks exactly four miles away—that house all the extras. As the darkness deepens, pale globes begin to glow above the street. Eventually two people emerge from the cafe. Dominique has her hand in the crook of Ahmed's arm. They stroll along the sidewalk. The Hudson Terraplane demurely follows.

All this time Ahmed has been talking. His exact words are not important. He has mentioned truth and beauty. He has discussed film as a higher order of reality. All realities, he argued, were creations. What was left out was just as important as what was included. This was as true in life, he said, as it was in film. He called attention to the small engine attached, like a succubus, to the right side of the Indian motorcycle. On the screen this engine would never be seen; hence one could say it did not exist. But wasnt the absence of the engine, which at least worked, as significant as the presence of the engine which didnt? Wasnt the *unseen* as real as the *seen?* His dark hands waved in the air. Occasionally they dipped to Dominique's leg. Like her legs, her lips were slightly parted. The lips seemed fuller than before. Perhaps she has added lipstick. She wore, and continues to wear, her twilight dress. She will wear it, or a copy of it—three have been made for her—for the rest of the film and the rest of this book. She will also wear her patent leather shoes, iridescent in this dim light. The shoes have very high, stiletto heels. Her black nylon stockings—perhaps they are silk—have seams down their backs. All during the rest of this book, and the movie, her thighs above these stockings will be soft and faintly moist. When opportunities arise, Ahmed will slide his hands up these legs, along the slick nylon encasing them, to the moist thighs. These opportunities will be described as they occur.

She walks, her hand in the crook of Ahmed's arm, with the same liquid grace as Ahmed. This liquid grace is admirable. We admire it, just as we admire the purring Hudson Terraplane that follows them down this Ethiopian street.

14. It is dark, perhaps very dark. But the darkness is ameliorated by the lamps set around the courtyard of Haile Selassie's summer palace. The Hudson Terraplane has come to a halt in this courtyard. The chauffeur—portrayed by Dar bin Saleh, who was, or will be, murdered behind the Hotel Savoy—opens the door for Dominique, who slides her legs out, and then for Ahmed, whose face gives no sign of recognition. Dominique and Ahmed walk through aromatic air, past blossoming citrus and night-blooming jasmine, and enter the palace. Their walk continues inside the palace. It is not our intention to describe this walk in great detail. It takes the two of them, at their stately pace, a considerable length of time to reach our next scene. The palace, built in the grand days of Haile Selassie's reign, is gigantic. Each hallway runs in a cardinal direction. Slaves stand, rather like storks, at regular intervals, holding hyena-tail fans. The floors are marble, quarried from the Rift Valley. Dominique's heels tap on these floors. During the course of this walk they pass two black panthers attended by boys in white caftans, and three lion cubs playing in the intersection of two hallways. One of these hallways is hung with copies—we imagine they are copies—of the Black Paintings by Francisco Goya. *Saturn Devouring His Son* is prominently displayed. The stately walk of Dominique and Ahmed does not falter—her right hand in the crook of his left arm—as they pass this gruesome work.

There is no need to continue this description. Tapestries cover many of the walls, illustrating scenes of Ethiopian life. Artists like Mali, Cheboya, and Keto spent their lives in this palace designing these tapestries. Looms hummed day and night. Artisans created the bejeweled chandeliers using gold originally mined from Ophir, whose location is now forgotten. Court painters filled entire rooms with masterpieces never seen outside Ethiopia. Many of these resemble the Black Paintings of Goya in their morbidity. Others are frankly erotic. Only a few are playful—Ethiopian artists are seldom playful. The walk of Dominique and Ahmed beside these works of art is just as striking, in its own way, as the art itself. Perhaps they are themselves works of art.

They come at last to a large room. The room is large enough so it could be used—in a film, for instance—as the setting for a nightclub or restaurant. A giant Panavision camera stands to one side. Prester John waits next to it. Elsewhere in the room the Queen of Sheba, as low to the ground as a hyena, examines a jewel-encrusted icon. In one corner, surrounded by the six Princesses of the Court, is Haile Selassie, or George Smithers. On a dais is an old lion. His pelt suffers from mange. Flies circle him, landing occasionally in his eyes, which then blink. Standing outside—he is visible through the open doors—is John Twelve. He is at the parapet, looking down over the Valley of Shoa. He wears his black silk robe. There is a lion embroidered in gold thread on the back of this robe. This lion looks healthier than the lion on the dais.

A discussion takes place at dinner. All sit at a long table. The first topic of conversation is The Agony of Ethiopia. Following this is The Disequilibrium of the West, The Corruption of Beauty, The Desolation of the Human Spirit, and The Apotheosis of John Twelve.

The behavior of the twelve people at the table during these discussions is worth noting. Haile Selassie and his six Princesses of the Court are to our left. The six Princesses are all between the ages of ten and twelve. Each has budding breasts and has experienced the menses at least once. They wear tight black skirts and black patent shoes with high heels. Sometimes they sit. More often, as the conversation progresses, they cluster around Haile Selassie. Selassie's tiny hands—like silver fish—dart into their clothing. The girls giggle and jump. He puts morsels into their mouths. They put their hands over his eyes and whisper into his ear. Haile Selassie pays no attention to the conversation at the table. Haile Selassie has become senile. This was apparent during the last years of his reign. He spent more time putting his hands up the skirts of his Princesses than he did on affairs of state. The Princesses did not seem to mind this—they competed among themselves for his attention—but the country fell on harsh times. Rivers dried up. The desert spread. The famous gum trees of Addis Ababa, which Selassie himself had caused to be planted, were chopped down for firewood. With no one keeping an eye on the treasury, greed became unchecked. Government officials drove increasingly huge cars and began keeping many mistresses. Selassie's edicts became erratic. He only wanted to play with his Princesses, who loved him so, and he resented the questions his ministers kept bringing him. The Princesses entertained him even after he was deposed, although by then they existed only in his imagination. He loved their satiny little breasts with the hard little nubbins at their tips. He loved the way they squealed when his tiny fingers nibbled, like fish, at their orifices. He grinned happily. He wore splendid uniforms with lots of gold braid and he had never felt so loved.

❖

While Haile Selassie plays with his Princesses, Prester John, on the far right, gets up to check his Panavision camera.

Crab meat, piles of yeasty bread, and asparagus soup steam on the table. The camera, guided by Prester John, records all of it. In preparation for *The Ethiopian Exhibition*, Prester John studied cinematography for a year at a university in Southern California. Since he lost his faith in Jesus, nothing else has so excited him. Although he does not talk about it—he still will not speak—he understands film is the perfect metaphor for the modern world. Everything had become superficial—a micromillimeter deep. Television, of course, was even better in this respect than film, but Prester John could not stand the blown-dry hairdos and the rictus-smiles of the men and women who worked in television. Film was more ambiguous, because, although it could be as superficial as television, it could also strip layer after layer off the modern life he despised. He saw modern life as being composed of layers of falsehoods. When you stripped off one lie you discovered one more below it. Below this lie was yet another. If all the layers were stripped away, what would be left? Nothing? The truth? Or the biggest, most grotesque lie of all? The pursuit of this engrossed him. Perhaps, he sometimes imagined, the central lie was Jesus. Or God. He grinned secretly at this possibility.

The university where he studied cinematography was very expensive. Nevertheless it was surrounded on three sides by a black ghetto. Twelve times Prester John strolled through this ghetto. On seven of these occasions he was mugged. Sometimes he gave his muggers money—he always kept a few dollars on him—and his wrist watch, which didnt work anyway. Sometimes he merely smiled at the muggers and continued on his way. What could muggers do to a dead Ethiopian king? Other times, when he felt irritable, he drove them off. He boxed their ears. He kicked them. If he'd had his sword—how he missed his sword!—he'd have chopped them to pieces. But his rage dissipated quickly. Mostly he was amused. He was amused that the female students at this university, after paying their expensive tuition, had to be escorted by burly male guards to their dorms and the parking lots. This was an effort to keep them from being raped. The notion of raping one of these pale, insipid creatures was amusing also. Sometimes he wondered if he himself should rape one of them. Would the experience be as superficial as he imagined? In his mind he created the camerawork necessary for such a scene. He also panned over the jewel-like campus, past the keen-faced engineering students planning the future of the world, and slipped into the dark streets surrounding, where no future existed. The camera in his head was forever busy. Since he eschewed words, he thought in images. He saw faces that looked like BMWs. He saw faces that looked as raw as uncooked heroin. He saw eyes that looked like the barrels of rifles. He saw a whole city dissolving in its own acid. He thought these images were lovely.

Sheba sits next to Prester John. It is said—although perhaps this is legend, and not truth—that once she was beautiful. Certainly she had courage. As a young Queen she made the arduous journey from Ethiopia to Israel: she had heard of the great King Solomon and wanted to know him. She was already tired of Ethiopian men. She was tired of men who lied. She was tired of men who were stupid. She was tired of flatulent men, and vain men, and men who wore out before she did. There was already something feral about her. Her lower jaw was slung forward, so her teeth always showed. Just by staring at a man who displeased her she could make his legs collapse. But perhaps she was beautiful. She journeyed to Israel, beautiful or not, with camels weighted down with gold and spices and jewels. She carried jasper and sapphire, chalcedony and emerald, sardonyx, sardus, and chrysolite, fine beryl and topaz, chests of chrysoprase, jacinth, and amethyst, and, of course, the finest jewel of all—herself. Solomon had never seen such riches.

"Solomon!" she brayed once to Ahmed. "What an asshole!" What a disappointment. His buttocks, she claimed, were wider than her own, which were wide enough, even then. A paunch drooped over his penis, which was indiscriminate in its attentions. His famous wisdom was nothing but primitive shrewdness laced with sadism. Perhaps Sheba's memory is faulty. This was three thousand years ago. Her hips now are like the haunches of a hyena. Her head hangs forward, like the head of a hyena. Solomon had praised her pomegranate cheeks, but her cheeks now are hairy and mottled. All that honey and cream! she cries. God, was I sick of myrrh and aloe! Was her navel a goblet filled with wine? Were her breasts like fawns? Perhaps. But *his* kisses were not sweet as wine, they were sour like yesterday's arak. His famous temple was shabby—his palace even worse. The Israelites themselves were a flatulent lot, perhaps because of their strange diet. And their god! He condemned this, he condemned that, just like a man! When she menstruated she had to go into a special room in Solomon's palace and stay there for seven days. That was humiliating for a woman who considered her body's blood as valuable as rubies, her effluvium as rich as diamonds. "What an asshole!" she brays.

She returned to Ethiopia and took solace in sardonyx and chalcedony. She spent hours examining rubies. Amethyst and topaz were woven into her hair. When she needed a man, which became less and less frequently, she bought one with a gem. In recent centuries she particularly liked poor Spanish boys. There seemed an unending supply of them. They would do anything for her gems. They were pretty to look at, too. They were as pretty as jasper, although they didnt last as long. They had pretty eyes, pretty hands, pretty feet. Sometimes this roused her envy. Her own feet were yellowed and callused. Her hands had fat, yellow fingers. Her eyes were yellow, too. Once to see what a pretty Spanish boy would take from her, she inserted twenty-four large rubies into his rectum. His smile grew wider with each gem. At the twenty-fourth his face suddenly paled. Blood poured from between his pomegranate buttocks. Nevertheless he continued to smile. When she left him, he was all white and red and still, but the smile remained on his face. She was grinning, too, lips drawn back from her yellow stubs of teeth.

On the dais the lion stirs. He snaps at a fly, yawns, and settles his head again between his paws. Ahmed nods towards him.

"Once," he tells Dominique, "lions were plentiful in Ethiopia. Great lions, virile lions."

"What happened?"

"They were hunted to extinction, of course."

All conversations take place on two or more levels. This one is no exception. Ahmed was also saying—although these words were never uttered, but lay beneath the surface—that only man was crueler than the great cats. But everyone knew that. Everyone acknowledged, for instance, Ahmed said beneath the surface, the horror of war. Yet wars occurred with great regularity. Increasingly efficient weapons killed increasingly large numbers of people. Great multitudes of men and women worked for living wages producing bombs, bullets, missiles, barrels, breechlocks, stocks, mortars, gunsights, tank turrets, cannons, troop carriers, shells and shell casings, poison gases, revolvers, carbines, automatics, and innumerable other instruments of destruction. More people yet paid money—pennies, nickels, dimes, dollars, rupees, shekels, rubles, pesos, pesetas, lire, dirhams, rials, zlotys, francs, balboas, rands—into the coffers of governments which converted that money into acts and instruments of destruction. All this was done daily, hourly, by the minute, by night as well as by day, on weekends and on holidays. That in itself was horrible. What was even more horrible, Ahmed said, or implied, was that all of us were capable of such acts of destruction. It was in our nature. All of us, he said, are murderers. There is no cruel or despicable act ever done by any human being, anywhere, that I am incapable of doing myself. And you.

No, not I, protested Dominique.

Yes, you. Me. All of us. It is our nature.

That would be too horrible—

We do not judge nature, my dear. Nature is the standard by which we are judged. And nature has decreed our cruelty. There can be no other explanation for the history of our race. I myself have felt every stirring of greed, every perversion, every hatred. It is impossible to be a human being and not be cruel. To claim otherwise is a contradiction of terms.

I dont believe—

Only one thing makes this bearable, Ahmed continues beneath their other conversation. Humans are also the most creative creatures on earth. No other creature has this power to the same degree. There are only three events of importance in human existence, Dominique, and these events repeat themselves, metaphorically, throughout our lives. There is birth, which is creation in its purest form. There is death, which is the ultimate destruction. And there is sex, which combines both creation and destruction into a single act. Can this be doubted? A man's organ penetrates into a woman's womb in exactly the same way a spear penetrates the thorax. There is thrusting, and more thrusting. The weapon twists, cruelly. It withdraws, dripping blood—or semen. All the words which describe an act of sex may be used to describe an act of violence. An orgasm is like death. Yet such is the alchemical nature of sex that this act of violence is turned into creation. Only a woman can do this for a man. Her body absorbs his. His weapon is taken. His thrusting is accepted. The agony of destruction is joined immutably to the agony of creation. It is alchemy. It is the alchemy of art. It is the same transmutation that the artist achieves in his work. Death and creation become one. They become transcendent. Only this, Dominique, allows a man and a woman to truly live. Without this a man walks in desolation. He is a warrior dying in the desert. Without this a civilization can only destroy. That is the desolation of our modern world. We are out of balance, Dominique. We are warriors dying in a desert. We are warriors walking in desolation, dying in the desert.

Dominique's face has gone pale. With his fingers Ahmed touches her face as gently as the wing of a bird touches the wind.

"That is why," he says, "you are my love. My salvation. My hope."

❖

At the center of the table John Twelve lifts his head. His face is pale, too. There is sweat on his skin.

"Listen," he says. "They are coming."

His face is pale with fear. Fear is visible in every line. Yet there is something else. There is something else in his face. It is glory. This glory illuminates him. As the light in the room grows dim, this glory in John Twelve's face seems almost luminescent.

15. It is dark. Below them, however—below the summer palace of Haile Selassie—there is light. Everyone except Haile Selassie and his Princesses gathers at the parapet. They watch the lights moving below. They listen to the songs rising from below.

In the darkness the town is not visible below the summer palace of Haile Selassie. Even we cannot see it. If we were an Ethiopian bird, however—or the camera in the head of Prester John—we could rise off the parapet of the palace and swoop down through the black air. We could glide to the square far below. In this square people are milling. They carry torches. It is these torches which the people above can see. These torches circle right and left. More torches emerge from the darkness, from the dark streets which have been created around the central square. Some of these torches are carried by blind children. Translucent skin has grown over their eye sockets. They are led by children who have single eyes and as many as fifteen fingers. All are dressed in black. Children with no legs and mere fins for arms are carried by children with hydroencephalic heads. Julio Abril, in his mauve dress and his Charles Jourdan shoes, mingles with them. His pointed tongue flicks at his painted lips. He has just received a new injection of lamb embryo, and has never felt so feminine. A Nazi, or someone playing a Nazi in jackboots and peaked cap, eyes him invitingly. The shadows thrown by his torch linger over the bodies of Dankalis, thin savages, nearly naked, who dance at the edges of the group.

The murdered Dar bin Saleh, in his chauffeur's uniform, raises his torch and cries out. He starts up the road which leads from the plaza to the summer palace of Haile Selassie. The engineers and surveyors who helped build this road saunter along the side, carrying their clipboards. They comment caustically on the quality of work and material that were used on the road. The laborers themselves follow behind, many of them drunk. Tourists are clustered in the center of the road. Each carries a camera and traveler's checks. They are tall, somewhat fleshy people, wearing flowered shirts. They have slack jaws and eyes that are withdrawn, protectively. At the tail end of this group are teenaged American girls, many of them bloodstained. Black children pluck at the tourists.

"Money!" they cry.

"Money!"

"Money!"

Their thin black hands dart into pockets. They wave wallets, keyrings, coins, and traveler's checks in the air like trophies. The tourists slap at their clothes, slap at the boys, and mill protectively together. All of them move up the road, illuminated by torches which burn like hot red eyes in the darkness.

John Twelve moves closer to the edge of the parapet. For a moment his black robe billows behind him. Then he pulls it closed.

"Wont someone help me?" he whispers.

Prester John turns busily to his camera. Sheba inspects the rings on one of her hands. In the other room, though visible through the open door, the lion on his dais yawns and shakes his head. Dominique turns to Ahmed, who puts up a hand. There is no one to help John Twelve. His face is waxen. With an effort he steadies himself. In the other room a Princess giggles, loudly, as Haile Selassie's fingers, like fish, nibble at one of her apertures.

"I'm sorry," John Twelve says. "I'm all right now."

His gaze falls to the scene below. Outside the camera's range, Ahmed watches.

❖

The same wind that whips John Twelve's robe around his bare ankles now makes the flames of the torches roar and sputter.

These torches cast their glow beyond the road's edge. Visible beyond the road's edge are oil cans, a dead dog, plastic bags and cups, leather shoes whose soles hang open like mouths, broken glass which sparkles in the light, soiled disposable diapers and menstrual pads, scraps of toilet paper fluttering in the wind, red and white milk cartons, and at least one empty box of texturized soya protein. The hooves of a white pony—ridden by a black Abyssinian—dance among this detritus. Pariah dogs, running at the outskirts of the crowd, stick their noses into the plastic, paper, and leather oddments. An Ethiopian poet, skinny and effete, sneers at this and composes in his head an ironic couplet. We will spare our readers.

The cameras, mounted on giant hydraulic devices, swirl overhead. Fat policemen on Harley-Davidson motorcycles— cleaned and polished for the occasion—glance up at them and straighten their leather jackets. Other policemen in pale green uniforms march up the road. They pass a kneeling Julio

Abril, practicing his craft on the ersatz Nazi, and the old women beggars who squat in the shadows, counting beads. These women wear T-shirts with the names of rock groups printed on them. We can see REO Speedwagon, The Boss, Beatlemania, Stones In Concert, and even Fang, his incisors dripping blood. Just beyond them a whore wears a Mickey Mouse T-shirt. It is all she wears. Her breasts flap within this T-shirt and her belly, round and scarred, rises below it. Three drunken Ethiopians, holding each other up, stagger towards her, grinning. They leave behind them a trail of beer cans. A single camera swoops down to focus tightly on the whore's face. There is something beatific about her. Her eyes look beyond the drunk Ethiopians descending on her. She feels something more than their hands groping at her thighs. Perhaps she feels the tumors growing and pulsing within her abdomen. A great warmth spreads outward from her. Her eyes seem focused on something far, far distant, perhaps so far distant that no one else can see it. The camera lingers as she assumes the position of her trade, and the first drunk Ethiopian settles over her.

From above, the road seems a river of fire. From this river of fire a song emerges. It is sung by children waving flags. It is sung by children crawling on the pavement. A band plays, drums thumping, wind instruments wailing. By the time the song travels upward to the parapet where John Twelve is poised, the song is as soft as the breast of an Ethiopian bird. As the river of fire curls left, then right, mounting the hill to the summer palace of Haile Selassie, the song becomes stronger—though no less soft—and then weaker, though still beautiful. Everyone can hear it. A sound technician—perhaps he has been here all this time—sits at a bank of toggle switches and dials. Earphones are on his head. He leans forward and moves a switch, slides a lever, and taps thought-fully at a dial. The lion walks through the doorway and onto the parapet, where he sits, licking at his mangy fur. The sound technician ignores him.

"How much longer?" says John Twelve.

"Minutes," says Ahmed.

Dominique stares from one to the other. She sees John Twelve's robe flapping at his bare ankles. She sees Ahmed standing to one side, his face immobile. She edges away from the lion and puts a hand between her breasts. From the other room comes a burst of laughter. The sound technician raises an eyebrow. He scowls into his bank of instruments.

16. It is dark. It is very dark. The full moon is behind dark clouds. Yet in spite of this the glory on the face of John Twelve is visible. The glory is just as visible as the fear. The fear is just as visible as the sweat dripping down his face. His arms are raised. The wind whips his black robe away from his nude body. The robe flaps like a cape. It flaps like black wings from his shoulders.

The others on this parapet are visible also, although they are not lit from within. Dominique stands roughly equidistant between Ahmed and John Twelve, that is, about five paces from each. Her makeup is immaculate, as though applied specifically for this occasion. There is a gloss to her scarlet lips. There is a gloss, in fact, to her face, which turns one way—towards Ahmed—and then the other, towards John Twelve. The lips of Dominique are slightly parted, although at this moment the expression is not seductive but anguished. They are nonetheless tender. Even at this moment one might imagine—Ahmed, for instance, might imagine—kissing them with one's own lips. Like all American girls she has small, fine teeth, though whether or not this is the result of expensive orthodontics is unclear. Her legs, sheathed in taut nylon, are as beautiful as ever. Like her eyes, they turn nervously—first towards Ahmed, then towards John Twelve. All her movements are indecisive.

The clouds part. Prester John, taking advantage of the

moon's illumination, steps to his camera and makes last minute adjustments. It may be that his face, normally fierce, is softened by the moonlight. Beyond him, nearly obscured by a shadow, stands Sheba. Her head is lowered. Her yellow eyes stare, like the expressionless eyes of a scavenger, at John Twelve. Near her the lion moves restlessly. His tail switches from side to side. The bones and muscles move under his skin. The sound man, at his bank of instruments, seems bored. He listens through his instruments to the sounds of arc lights turning on in the distant rooms of Haile Selassie's summer palace.

These arc lights turn on with a *clang!* The lights are so powerful the people in these rooms stop. For a moment they mill about. Even the blind children seem pained by the light. Another light *clangs* on. Cameras are whirring overhead. Pressed from behind, by the great mass of people, the children, led by Dar bin Saleh, spill forward.

We have already described the rooms through which they pass, and the slaves, who stand one legged, like storks, at regular intervals. None of this has changed. Some of the tourists stop to admire the paintings in one hallway. A construction worker, elsewhere, tries to pry loose jewels encrusted to a statue. The hooves of a delicate Abyssinian pony rattle on the marble floor, rather like the stiletto heels of Julio Abril. Each time the children enter a room or pass into a new hallway, the giant arc lights come on with a *clang!* A new camera begins to whir. Cameras swoop down from the ceiling. Cameras on rails race past the hurrying figures. Black children chanting "Money! money! money!" swing off to the right, down an empty corridor, searching for items to steal. Others, men and women, old and young, including a slow moving beggar woman who counts her beads with each step, go astray by accident. Some of them will be in the palace, still lost, for years to come. The palace is huge. Some rooms are designed as mazes. People circle there, endlessly. Odalisques from another era lie on mats, their flesh as opalescent as pearls. There are thousands of slaves, stables filled with black and white horses, and lions who roam free in the deepest passages. All this still exists. The cameras and the arc lights do not go to these parts of Haile Selassie's summer palace.

Dar bin Saleh and the deformed children burst into a room large enough to be used as a nightclub. Arc lights—three of them—*clang! clang! clang!* White light bounces off the walls. Haile Selassie, or George Smithers, looks up, bewildered. One of his hands is in the skirt of a Princess. Her hands are at her face, hiding her mouth, which is giggling.

On the parapet Ahmed nods.

"Theyre here," he says.

"Theyre here," says John Twelve.

His lips are drawn back, revealing incisors that look like fangs.

❖

A bird floats high overhead. His beak is hooked. He is an Ethiopian bird of prey. His talons lay flat against his feathers. As he banks to one side—he is circling above Haile Selassie's summer palace—he sees arc lights spring to life. He even hears them: *clang! clang! clang!* This does not disturb his slow circling high overhead.

From this vantage, Prester John's camera can be seen to be in constant motion. It moves forward as children—blind, deformed—burst onto the parapet of Haile Selassie's summer palace. Then the camera swoops into the air, imitating—but not equaling—the flight of an Ethiopian bird. At the very edge of the parapet stands a figure in a black flapping robe. Five paces from him is a woman in a twilight-colored dress. Five paces further stands a dark, wiry Abyssinian. These three people are quite still. Then, pushed by those crowding behind, the children spill forward. They can be seen spreading out, in a fan shape, over the parapet. Yet even then the three figures we have mentioned do not move. Seconds pass, perhaps several seconds. The wind, which has been plucking, plucking at the robe of the man at the edge of the parapet, at last pulls it free. It slips from the man's shoulders. From our vantage high above, it looks like a bird suddenly released. The black wings of this bird-like robe flap over the heads of the advancing children, over Dar bin Saleh, over beggars and drunkards and thieves and liars, past a preening Julio Abril, past fat policemen sweating on their motorcycles, past a whore who limps, her eyes focused on eternity, and into the throat of a giant tuba which falls abruptly silent. The thin man, red and bony, stands naked at the edge of the parapet.

Perhaps he moves back. From above he seems to falter—to collapse a little. Perhaps his weight shifts backwards. At that moment the dark Abyssinian appears to make a gesture. This gesture is not seen clearly from our position. The woman, whether in response to this gesture or not, takes three steps towards the man at the parapet. The light must be blinding. Her hand goes up. The man at the edge of the parapet spreads his arms and dives off the edge.

❖

Prester John's camera sees the same things as our Ethiopian bird of prey, but adds a few details. When the lights *clang! clang! clang!* Sheba becomes visible in a corner, hissing between her yellowed teeth. Her face itself is yellow, hairy, and mottled. Other faces are also seen more clearly. We see the faces of the deformed children, many of them confused. We see the face of Dar bin Salah, revengeful. We see the faces of thieves and drunks. The shadows of all these people race over the parapet and over each other, cast in three directions by the three arc lights. This adds more confusion to the scene.

The black robe flaps and, like a shadow, frees itself from the man at the edge of the parapet. It sails over heads, through doors, and into the next room. The man at the edge of the parapet, now naked, is back-lit. A halo of light glows around his thin red body. Yet he now seems to falter. His shoulders hunch together. One foot gropes back from the edge of the precipice. At that point Ahmed—we see it clearly—lifts his hand. Dominique sees this, too. The lights blind her as she turns back towards John Twelve. Her eyes—tearful—flash as the light strikes her face. There are thousands of watts directed at her. Her eyes in this light are iridescent. Even her mouth, partly open, glows. Her dress luminesces. She cannot see John Twelve's eyes. We can. The glory has drained away, replaced with fear. But when he sees this glowing woman, one hand raised, his features lose their tension. The glory returns. His head lifts. Dominique, blinded, cannot see the effect she has on him. Her eyes are flashing like diamonds. Her mouth is like a ruby. Her dress glows like a sapphire. John Twelve, or Fang, raises his arms from his naked body. The edge of the parapet seems to crumble. He leans forward into the darkness.

The lights *clang! clang! clang!* Shadows race everywhere. The woman, in response to her cue, steps forward three paces. Her beauty and mystery are unmistakable. Her entire body is radiant. John Twelve, or Fang, who has dreamed forever of this radiance, steps to the edge of the precipice. His robe has already flown from his shoulders and over the heads of the deformed, the cruel, the terrible creatures who press towards him. He leans into a darkness made radiant by beauty. He leans, naked, into a darkness made beautiful by radiance. The precipice crumbles beneath him.

The lights hiss as they cool. People talk, complaining about the food, the weather, the long hours. Their heels tap on the marble floors. More lights turn off, and begin to hiss. We hiss, too, as the summer palace of Haile Selassie is emptied.

17. It is dark, perhaps very dark. Yet in this darkness is visible a woman. She sits on the edge of a bed. Her hair seems thicker and longer than when last we saw her. Her eyes, though still hooded, are deeper. Over her shoulders is a black silk robe. Her slender legs are placed carefully before her. All this is barely visible in the black, black air.

Morning comes. A sea, to the east, reddens. The streets of the town fill with murderers and thieves, with petty cheats and foolish liars. Garbage litters the gutters, where dogs slink from shadow to shadow. Men drop their feces in alleys. Cracks spread across concrete walls. Pavement buckles, as though the earth itself heaved. The sun blazes down on all of it. It blazes through the window and into the room where the woman sits. At last she moves. She moves wearily, but with exquisite grace, to the window. Her robe is open, thus revealing to us her long thighs, the little patch of hair between them, her flat stomach, the still young breasts. At the window she stares down into a daytime world in which everything is visible. There are no mysteries in the harsh shadows. There is no radiance in this harsh glare. In the harsh light nothing luminesces. The woman turns away. She moves with her weary grace across the room. With her eyes lowered she examines her face in a mirror. She touches one breast. Then she goes to her purse, which lies open on the bed.

Within this purse are tickets. It is not clear how they came to be there. There are bus tickets, first, second, and third class train tickets, tickets good for journeys on coastal steamers, and airplane tickets to destinations throughout the world. Some of these tickets would return her to the country and the city from whence she came. Many would take her to places she has never been. Some of them—we are not certain how many—would take her to Ahmed. He is waiting, in another place. None of the tickets include return journeys. They are all one way. That is one of the peculiarities of Ethiopia. In Ethiopia, a journey once taken, can never be undone, just as the Ethiopian night, once glimpsed, can never be forgotten. Restlessly, restlessly, the woman moves from the bed to the window to the mirror, while outside the sun blazes across the sky. As it dips towards the horizon we can see the shadows lengthen. Perhaps there is a distant murmur. Perhaps there is a suggestion of luminescence—of radiance—to the air. It cannot quite be seen. Nevertheless we have faith it is there. We have faith she will see it. Night will come. In Ethiopia, night will always come. We will wait for it, just as we wait for her, faithfully.

THE BLACK ICE BOOKS SERIES

The Black Ice Books Series introduces readers to the new generation of dissident writers in revolt. Breaking out of the age-old traditions of mainstream literature, the voices published here are at once ribald, caustic, controversial, and inspirational. These books signal a reflowering of the art underground. They explore iconoclastic styles that celebrate life vis-a-vis the spirit of their unrelenting energy and anger. Similar to the recent explosion in the alternative music scene, these books point toward a new counter-culture rage that's just now finding its way into the mainstream discourse.

The Kafka Chronicles
A novel by Mark Amerika
The Kafka Chronicles investigates the world of passionate sexual experience while simultaneously ridiculing everything that is false and primitive in our contemporary political discourse. Mark Amerika's first novel ignites hyper-language that explores the relationship between style and substance, self and sexuality, and identity and difference. His energetic prose uses all available tracks, mixes vocabularies, and samples genres. Taking its cue from the recent explosion of angst-driven rage found in the alternative rock music scene, this book reveals the unsettled voice of America's next generation.

Mark Amerika has lived in Florida, New York, California, and different parts of Europe, and has worked as a free-lance bicycle courier, lifeguard, video cameraman, and greyhound racing official. Amerika's fiction has appeared in many magazines, including *Fiction International, Witness,* the German publication *Lettre International*, and *Black Ice*, of which he is editor. He is presently writing a "violent concerto for deconstructive guitar" in Boulder, Colorado.

"Mark Amerika not only plays music—the rhythm, the sound of his words and sentences—he plays verbal meanings as if they're music. I'm not just talking about music. Amerika is showing us that William Burroughs came out of jazz knowledge and that now everything's political—and everything's coming out through the lens of sexuality..."

—*Kathy Acker*

Paper, ISBN: 0-932511-54-6, $7.00

Revelation Countdown
Short Fiction by Cris Mazza

While in many ways reaffirming the mythic dimension of being on the road already romanticized in American pop and folk culture, *Revelation Countdown* also subtly undermines that view. These stories project onto the open road not the nirvana of personal freedom, but rather a type of freedom more closely resembling loss of control. Being in constant motion and passing through new environments destabilizes life, casts it out of phase, heightens perception, skews reactions. Every little problem is magnified to overwhelming dimensions; events segue from slow motion to fast forward; background noises intrude, causing perpetual wee-hour insomnia. In such an atmosphere, the title *Revelation Countdown*, borrowed from a roadside sign in Tennessee, proves prophetic: It may not arrive at 7:30, but revelation will inevitably find the traveler.

Cris Mazza is the author of two previous collections of short fiction, *Animal Acts* and *Is It Sexual Harassment Yet?* and a novel, *How to Leave a Country*. She has resided in Brooklyn, New York; Clarksville, Tennessee; and Meadville, Pennsylvania; but she has always lived in San Diego, California.

"...fictions that are remarkable for the force and freedom of their imaginative style."

—*New York Times Book Review*

Paper, ISBN: 0-932511-73-2, $7.00

Damned Right

A novel by Bayard Johnson

Damned Right is a visceral new incarnation of the American road novel. Its twentysomething protagonist practices the religion of speed and motion, judging his every action by one question: Is it right? The freeways beyond his home in the Pacific Northwest call to him with their promise of a wide-open throttle and infidels to outrun. In a mountain community hard against the Canadian border, he attempts to save the life of a dying infant. This child forces a question into his heart, and, without fully understanding his mission, he is compelled to head south to discover the answer. The bleak sprawl of Los Angeles, a city of idealists imprisoned by their own fossilized dreams, lies ahead of him, drawing him into a series of adventures and ordeals and revealing to him an apocolyptic vision of the future.

Bayard Johnson has written more than sixty short stories, five movies, and over 220 songs. Three of his stage plays have been produced in small theaters in Los Angeles. Early in 1993, Johnson and AIM activist Russell Means formed Treaty Productions, with the intent of producing motion pictures promoting equality, brotherhood, and justice.

When you hunker down with this book *Damned Right* you better buckle-up seat belt, don crash helmet. You are gonna be propelled, rocketed, eye-balled down high-ways and fast-tracks of this low-writing speed-freak name of Bayard Johnson....He's a reckless rider swerving words under the influence of semantic juices Kerouac never dreamed of!"

—*Dr. Timothy Leary*

Paper, ISBN, : 0-932511-84-8, $7.00

Avant-Pop:
Fiction for a Daydream Nation

Edited by Larry McCaffery

In *Avant-Pop*, Larry McCaffery has assembled a collection of innovative fiction, comic book art, illustrations, and other unclassifiable texts written by the most radical, subversive, literary talents of the postmodern new wave. The authors included here vary in background, from those with well-established reputations as cult figures in the pop underground (Samuel R. Delany, Kathy Acker, Ferret, Derek Pell, Harold Jaffe), and important new figures who have gained prominence since the late eighties (Mark Leyner, Eurudice, William T. Vollmann), to, finally, the most promising new kids on the block. *Avant-Pop* is meant to send a collective wake-up call to all those readers who spent the last decade nodding off, along with the rest of America's daydream nation. To those readers and critics who have decried the absence of genuinely radicalized art capable of liberating people from the bland roles and assumptions they've accepted in our B-movie society of the spectacle, *Avant-Pop* announces that reports about the death of a literary avant-garde have been greatly exaggerated.

Larry McCaffery's most recent books include *Storming the Reality Studio: A Casebook of Cyberpunk and Postmodern SF* and *Across the Wounded Galaxies: Interviews with Contemporary American SF Writers.*
Paper, ISBN: 0-932511-72-44, $7.00

New Noir
Stories by John Shirley
In *New Noir*, John Shirley, like a postmodern Edgar Allen Poe, depicts minds deformed into fantastic configurations by the pressure, the very weight, of an entire society bearing down on them. "Jody and Annie on TV," selected by the editor of *Mystery Scene* as "perhaps the most important story...in years in the crime fiction genre," reflects the fact that whole segments of zeitgeist and personal psychology have been supplanted by the mass media, that the average kid on the streets in Los Angeles is in a radical crisis of exploded self-image, and that life really is meaningless for millions. The stories here also bring to mind

Elmore Leonard and the better crime novelists, but John Shirley—unlike writers who attempt to extrapolate from peripheral observation and research—bases his stories on his personal experience of extreme people and extreme mental states, and his struggle with the seductions of drugs, crime, prostitution, and violence.

John Shirley was born in Houston, Texas in 1953, but spent the majority of his youth in Oregon. He has been a lead singer in a rock bank, Obsession, writes lyrics for various bands, including Blue Oyster Cult, and in his spare time records with the Panther Moderns. He is the author of numerous works in a variety of genres; his story collection *Heatseeker* was chosen by the Locus Reader's Poll as one of the best collections of 1989. His latest novel is *Wetbones*.

"John Shirley serves up the bloody heart of a rotting society with the aplomb of an Aztec surgeon on Dexedrine."

—*ALA Booklist*

Paper, ISBN: 0-932511-55-4, $7.00

The Ethiopian Exhibition
A novel by D.N. Stuefloten

While World War II rages in Europe, John Twelve climbs onto a four-cylinder Indian motorcycle and crosses Ethiopia, searching for truth, for beauty, for mystery. At the same time, a modern American girl strolls the streets of Puerto Vallarta, where she is accosted by a film director—actually Ahmed, an Ethiopian murderer. He is making a film, he explains, about a man crossing the Ethiopian desert on a motorcycle. The girl accepts a starring role—and with this embarks on an adventure that takes her beyond the limits of ordinary reality. Her companions on this mystery tour include Sheba, the 3,000-year-old Queen of Ethiopia; Prester John, the legendary King of Ethiopia; and the Emperor Haile Selassie, the Conquering Lion of Judah. The innocent American girl, now called Dominique, watches in amazement and alarm as the world reveals an esoteric reality that she never knew existed.

D.N. Stuefloten has spent most of his life wandering around the world writing novels. He has been a magician's assistant in Africa, the manager of a mining company in Borneo, a fisherman in the south seas, and a smuggler in India. His first novel, *Maya,* was published in 1992 by Fiction Collective Two. Paper, ISBN: 0-932511-85-6, $7.00

Doggy Bag
Stories by Ronald Sukenick

Doggy Bag is a contemporary answer to T.S. Eliot's "The Waste Land"—don't waste anything. It forges an Avant-Pop credo from recycled scraps of American mass culture. In the age of the consumer, the American tourists in this series of interconnected stories are still trying to buy answers in Europe, but finally they're forced to conclude that whatever they're looking for isn't there. These travelers must turn back to what they know best, sampling the entertainment industry, B-movie versions of ancient mythologies, urban myth, advertising, and popular lore. They communicate their findings through cryptograms, secret codes, and strange graphic designs. Along the way they encounter Federico Fellini, Jim Morrison, a bird named Edgar Allan Crow, a secret sect of White Voodoo Financial Wizards, humans infected with a computer virus, the Iron Sphincters, the Guardian Angel Mind Liberation Unit, the Wolfman, Total Control, Inc., and Bruno the sex dog, among other bizarre phenomena. The characters in these stories—from the New World in more senses than one—have no choice but to attempt to sort out a fresh spiritual commitment from the confused sound bites of a channel surfer's nightmare. They summon the reader to join a shadowy conspiracy in support of traditional American values of liberation and freedom.

Ronald Sukenick has previously published ten books, among them *Down and In, Up, and Blown Away.* He is the publisher of *American Book Review* and of *Black Ice* magazine, as well as codirector of Fiction Collective Two. He lives in Boulder, Colorado; New York; and Paris; and is a professor at the University of Colorado.

Paper, ISBN: 0-932511-82-1, $7.00

Individuals may order any or all of the Black Ice Book series directly from Fiction Collective Two, Publication Unit, Illinois State University, Campus Box 4241, Normal, IL 61790-4241. (Check or money order only, made payable to Fiction Collective Two.) Bookstore, library, and text orders must be placed through the distributor: The Talman Company, Inc., 131 Spring Street, #201 E-N, New York, NY 10012; Customer Service: 800/537-8894.